OSLG

D0368220

SPECIAL MESSAGE TO READERS

This book is published under the auspices of

THE ULVERSCROFT FOUNDATION

(registered charity No. 264873 UK)

Established in 1972 to provide funds for research, diagnosis and treatment of eye diseases. Examples of contributions made are: —

A Children's Assessment Unit at Moorfield's Hospital, London.

•

Twin operating theatres at the Western Ophthalmic Hospital, London.

•

A Chair of Ophthalmology at the Royal Australian College of Ophthalmologists.

•

The Ulverscroft Children's Eye Unit at the Great Ormond Street Hospital For Sick Children, London.

You can help further the work of the Foundation by making a donation or leaving a legacy. Every contribution, no matter how small, is received with gratitude. Please write for details to:

**THE ULVERSCROFT FOUNDATION,
The Green, Bradgate Road, Anstey,
Leicester LE7 7FU, England.
Telephone: (0116) 236 4325**

**In Australia write to:
THE ULVERSCROFT FOUNDATION,
c/o The Royal Australian and New Zealand
College of Ophthalmologists,
94-98 Chalmers Street, Surry Hills,
N.S.W. 2010, Australia**

ELOPING WITH EMMY

Emerald Carlisle's father will do anything to stop a wedding between her and her penniless friend Kit Fairfax. Announcing their engagement seems a sure-fire way of helping Kit raise some cash! Tom Brodie is her father's lawyer. His duty, to buy off the groom and to bring Emerald to heel, is thwarted by Emerald's beauty and charm. When she persuades him to help her 'elope', Tom soon realises she could persuade him to take her anywhere . . . even up the aisle!

Books by Liz Fielding
in the Linford Romance Library:

HIS LITTLE GIRL
GENTLEMEN PREFER . . .
BRUNETTES
DANGEROUS FLIRTATION
AN IMAGE OF YOU

LIZ FIELDING

ELOPING WITH EMMY

Complete and Unabridged

LINFORD
Leicester

First published in Great Britain in 1998

First Linford Edition
published 2009

Copyright © 1998 by Liz Fielding
All rights reserved

British Library CIP Data

Fielding, Liz.
    Eloping with Emmy. - -
    (Linford romance library)
    1. Love stories.
    2. Large type books.
    I. Title II. Series
    823.9'14–dc22

    ISBN 978–1–84782–945–0

Published by
F. A. Thorpe (Publishing)
Anstey, Leicestershire

Set by Words & Graphics Ltd.
Anstey, Leicestershire
Printed and bound in Great Britain by
T. J. International Ltd., Padstow, Cornwall

This book is printed on acid-free paper

1

Tom Brodie regarded the man sitting behind the ornate desk. It was the first time he had met Gerald Carlisle; clients of such importance were usually dealt with by partners with pedigrees as long as his own.

Brodie was the first to admit that he didn't have a pedigree of any kind. What he'd achieved in his thirty-one years had nothing to do with family background or the school he'd been to, it had been in spite of them.

It was the source of infinite satisfaction for him to know that one of the City's oldest law firms, the august legal partnership of Broadbent, Hollingworth & Maunsell, had been driven to offer him a partnership because of their desperate need for sharp new brains to drag them out of their Dickensian ways, bring their systems up to date and put them on track for the twenty-first century.

They'd tried offering him a consultancy. They'd tried a lump sum fee. He'd watched them wriggle with a certain detached amusement as they'd tried to buy his brains without having to take him and his working class background into their august establishment, well aware that they needed him far more than he needed them. Which was why he'd refused to consider anything but a full partnership.

One day, quite soon, he would insist that they add his name to the discreet brass plaque beside the shiny black front door of their offices. They wouldn't like that either. But they'd do it. The thought made listening to Gerald Carlisle's worries about his tiresome daughter almost bearable.

Gerald Carlisle was not his client. Brodie was too egalitarian in his principles, too forthright in his views to be let loose around a client who had a family tree with a tap root that reached down to the robber barons of the Middle Ages, with land and money as old. This didn't worry him. He had his own clients, companies run by men like himself who used their wits and their brains to create wealth instead of living off the past. Companies that brought in new money and big fees. It was the reason for his confidence about the brass plaque.

But today was the twelfth of August. When Carlisle's call for help had come through to the BHM offices, Tom had been the only partner at his desk. Everyone else had already packed their Purdeys and headed north for the grouse moors of their titled clients. It was tradition, apparently, and BHM, as Tom was constantly reminded, was a traditional firm with old-fashioned values which apparently included shooting birds in vast numbers in the middle of August.

Tradition also required that when a client of Gerald Carlisle's importance telephoned, he should speak to nothing less than a full partner, and so he had been put through to Tom Brodie.

Gerald Carlisle, however, did not wish to discuss business over the telephone, and so Tom had regretfully cancelled his dinner engagement with a delectable silver-blonde barrister with whom he had been playing kiss-chase for some weeks and driven to Lower Honeybourne.

Now, with the dusk gathering softly beyond the tall windows, he was sitting in the panelled study of Honeybourne Park, an impressive stone manor house set in countless acres of rolling Cotswold parkland, while Carlisle explained the urgency of his problem.

'Emerald has always been something of a handful,' he was saying. For 'handful', Brodie thought, read 'spoilt'. 'Losing her mother so young . . .'

Anyone would think, from Carlisle's hushed tones, that his wife had expired from some tragic illness rather than running away with a muscular polo player and leaving her young daughter to the tender ministrations of a series of nannies. She had been a bit of a 'handful' too — still was if the gossip columns were to be believed. Like mother, like daughter, apparently.

'I can see your problem, Mr Carlisle,' Tom said, his face blank of expression. He was well used to keeping his feelings to himself. 'I just don't understand what you want me to do about it.'

Upon hearing the man's proposed solution and the part he was expected to play in this, Brodie sincerely wished that he, too, had had some pressing engagement at the other end of the country that had taken him out of the office today.

'Won't your daughter object?' he asked.

'You don't have to concern yourself with my daughter, Brodie. I'll deal with her. All I want you to do is talk to this . . . gigolo . . . and find out how much it will take to buy him off.'

Buy him off. Beneath that smooth aristocratic exterior, Brodie decided, Gerald Carlisle was a bully. He didn't like bullies and for just a moment felt a surge of sympathy for Carlisle's daughter and for the young man she had declared it was her intention to marry. But only for a moment because he didn't doubt that she was a spoilt brat who was always having to be bailed out of trouble. Maybe for once she should be left to get on with it, stew in a broth of her own making . . .

For one giddy moment he was tempted to suggest such a strategy, just to see the look on Carlisle's face. But it wouldn't do. Emerald Carlisle was an old-fashioned heiress on the grand scale. He knew that because BHM managed her trust. Or rather Hollingworth did. Personally. It was that big. And even a man of Tom's egalitarian principles understood that a gigolo — he almost gagged on the word — could not be allowed to prosper at the expense of one of BHM's most valuable clients. At least not while he was responsible for her.

Carlisle pushed a file across the desk.

'You'll find everything you need to know about Fairfax in there.'

Tom opened the folder and glanced at the top sheet — a report on Kit Fairfax from an investigation company which, from the thickness of the file, had been extremely thorough. He wouldn't have expected anything else. It was a perfectly reputable company that his own firm used when necessary, and Hollingworth had undoubtedly recommended them to Carlisle.

He flicked through the papers, glanced at the black and white photographs of a man in his early twenties, his hair long and curling over his shoulders. He had a slightly distant expression, as if unaware of the extraordinarily pretty girl at his side, her arm looped through his, her head resting on his shoulder, although such an idea seemed extremely unlikely.

As unlikely as the idea of a man setting an investigation agency to watch his own daughter simply because he didn't much care for her boyfriend.

The whole business left Tom Brodie with a bad taste in his mouth, but as he closed the folder he made a determined effort to bury his own personal prejudices. Gerald Carlisle was simply concerned about his daughter, probably with good cause. Doubtless she was the target of all kinds of fortune hunters. 'And if Fairfax won't be bought off?' he asked.

'Everyone has a price, Brodie. Try a hundred thousand. It's a nice, round sum.' Roundish, Brodie thought. In the way that peanuts were roundish. The guy must surely know that Emerald Carlisle was worth millions? But maybe he wasn't that ambitious; maybe a 'roundish' payoff was all that Fairfax was after. But somehow that dreamy face didn't quite fit such a cynical scenario. Carlisle must have seen the doubt in Brodie's face. 'It's a pity Hollingworth is away; he knows what he's doing.'

Tom's glance flickered to the other man. 'Is this a regular occurrence?'

Carlisle stiffened. 'Emerald is rather gullible. She needs protecting from unscrupulous people who would take advantage of her.'

'I see.' Obviously it was.

'I doubt it, Brodie. I very much doubt it.' He made it sound as if having Emerald for a daughter was like bearing the world on his shoulders. Maybe it was time he let the girl make a few mistakes. The longer he protected her, the harder it would eventually become. But Carlisle did not want to hear that, and Tom wasn't there to offer 'agony aunt' advice. 'I'm relying on you to deal with this situation quickly and without any fuss. Do whatever you have to. Hollingworth — '

'I'm sure Mr Hollingworth would be more than happy to come back from Scotland if you prefer that he handle such a delicate matter,' Brodie interjected quickly. His own speciality was corporate law. Buying off an unsuitable husband was new territory for him, territory he was not anxious to explore.

9

But there was no escape. 'That would take too long. I want this settled and I want it settled quickly, before Emerald does something she'll regret. You're Hollingworth's partner and I'm relying on you to do whatever you have to to stop my daughter marrying this man.'

★ ★ ★

Emerald Carlisle was fuming. She was nearly twenty-three years old, for heaven's sake. Quite capable of making a rational decision about the rest of her life.

But not quite so capable of anticipating her father's ruthlessness when it came to getting his own way.

She grasped the doorknob in both hands and shook it furiously. It didn't budge. It was locked, and cursory examination of the keyhole revealed that the key had been removed. He had obviously foreseen the possibility that she might try poking it out of the lock onto a piece of paper. Assuming she had a piece of paper. She gave the door a kick, but it made no impression. It was still locked.

How dared her father lock her up in the nursery like some Victorian papa? Did he think she'd just sit quietly and take it?

Easily, was the answer to her first question. And, no. He knew she wouldn't take such treatment quietly, which was why he had tricked her into the second-floor nursery, conveniently equipped with safety bars across the window.

She abandoned the door and rushed across to the open window as she heard a car crunching over the gravel carriage drive that swept in front of the house, pulling herself up on the bars to get a better view.

It was a dark BMW, not a car she recognised, and it was parked too close to the house to get a good look at the driver as he climbed out. Just a glimpse of thick dark hair, a pair of wide shoulders as he shrugged into his jacket, a feeling that he was above average height, although with her foreshortened view from the second floor it was impossible to say for sure. From the expensive cut of his charcoal-grey suit it was obvious that he was some business connection of her father's, in which case he was definitely not the kind of person to whom she could appeal for help. She gave a little sigh.

It would have been so perfect if it had been Kit come to rescue her, driving up in his battered white van like some latter-day Galahad and hammering on the front door. But Kit was no Galahad. Kit had no idea what had happened. She hadn't dared tell him her plan or he would have been thoroughly shocked.

He was such a hopeless *dreamer*. Despite all his problems he'd packed his paints and taken off for France for the summer. At the time she'd been furious, but at least her father didn't know where to find him. Yet. But she had to get out of here before he did or her neat little plan would simply fall apart.

She had underestimated her father. She'd known he'd been having her followed, that was what had given her the idea in the first place. He was so *protective*. Which was why she'd known exactly what his response would be to her announcement that she planned to marry Kit . . .

Well, she mentally conceded, she hadn't known *exactly*. She certainly hadn't anticipated that he would lock her up like the heroine of some ridiculous melodrama or she would never have walked into his trap. He must have planned the whole thing after she'd telephoned to say she had to see him about something important. Her biggest mistake had been to put him on his guard, but it had been the only way of ensuring her father's attention. She twisted the small diamond engagement ring around her finger.

'Ooh!' she growled, venting her frustration on one of the bars fixed to the window frame to prevent small children from falling out by just the kind of careful Victorian papa she had been castigating, striking at it with a tight little fist. It shifted beneath the blow and she immediately forgot the pain caused by her temper. Instead she stared at the bar for a moment, then, slowly uncurling her fingers, she reached out and grasped it, giving it a sharp tug. She had not been mistaken; there was a small but quite positive movement.

Her spirits immediately began to rise and she looked about her for something to lever the horrid thing out of the frame. But the room was furnished with only a bed, a dresser, and a small hard-backed chair. And the built-in cupboard was bare, as she had already discovered to her disgust.

There was nothing in the least bit useful to be found, but she refused to be put off by this set-back. Instead, she returned to the window and gave the bar another, rather more vigorous shake. It was definitely loose, and, seized by the same enterprising spirit that had got her into this scrape in the first place, Emerald put her foot against the wall for leverage, took the bar in both hands and gave it a sharp tug. There was the promising sound of wood splintering against the screws, and, cheered by this success, she did it again, yanking on the bar with all her might until the window frame split with a satisfactory crack, disintegrating beneath the pressure and sending Emerald sprawling back on the floor, the bar still grasped tightly in her hands.

She stared at it for a moment in amazement, then she laughed out loud. The frame was rotten. It had rotted beneath the paintwork and no one had noticed. It was hardly surprising. The dreary old nursery hadn't been used since her grandfather was a baby, when children and servants had been expected to keep their proper place. Her mother had insisted on a bright, modern suite of rooms on the first floor for her baby girl, not that she'd hung around very long to enjoy them.

But Emerald didn't waste time congratulating herself on her luck, which was just as well, since even though the rest of the bars were dispensed with easily enough her problems were far from over. The nursery was on the second floor and there was the better part of fifty feet between her and the freedom of the gravel driveway.

It was a pity, she thought, that she had taken so much trouble dressing to create the right impression. Jeans and a pair of Doc Martens would have been far more practical for climbing down the ornate drainpipe than the elegant linen dress and high-heeled shoes she had decided would convince her father that she was serious. Her father, she knew, would never have taken her seriously in jeans, and it had been desperately important that he be convinced that she was in earnest. Unfortunately she had achieved her objective rather too well.

She considered the problem for a moment, then took off her shoes and dropped them out of the window onto the rose border below. She peeled off her stockings and, lacking a pocket in which to stow them, she stuffed them into her bra, because her high-heeled shoes would rub against her feet in five minutes without them and the last thing she needed right now was blisters.

She didn't have a handbag; she'd left it in the study when her father, brushing aside her declaration that she intended to marry a penniless artist, with or without his blessing, had asked her to give her opinion on some old toys that had been found in the attics during recent roof repairs.

After completing her fine arts degree, she had taken a job in an auction house where she had become fascinated with old toys. Her father had been furious that she had chosen to take a job at all, even one that any well-brought-up young heiress might covet. He had wanted her to stay at home, where he could keep an eye on her until he found her a suitable husband. Although she'd recognised the device was in the 'if we don't talk about it, it will go away' category, she had been sufficiently touched that he should have brought himself to acknowledge her expertise to fall for it.

She wasn't usually so gullible where her father was concerned, but with the lure of a lost hoard of Victorian toys discovered in a cupboard she had walked into the nursery without a suspicious thought in her head. That was when he had slammed the door and locked it behind her.

Pride, Emerald thought ruefully, always came before a fall. And of course there weren't any toys. If there had been, he would have summoned a *real* expert; he would certainly never have consulted his tiresome daughter.

Emerald gave the door a look that should have incinerated it. It wasn't even scorched, but in an attempt to slow down discovery of her flight she jammed the solitary chair beneath the doorknob. Then she hitched up her skirt and swung one leg over the window sill.

★　★　★

'I'll expect to hear from you within twenty-four hours that this matter has been settled, Brodie,' Carlisle was saying as he walked with him down the steps. 'I want no delay.'

'That should be all that it takes.' Brodie considered whether to mention the possibility that the lovebirds might already have flown, probably to one of those romantic destinations where weddings could be arranged in a matter of days, in which case it was already too late. But as they reached the bottom of the steps he decided against it. What clinched it was the sight of Emerald

Carlisle, her dress hitched up about her waist, clinging just above head height to an ornate lead drainpipe about twenty feet behind Gerald Carlisle's back.

Brodie knew that he should draw his client's attention to what was happening behind him. Something stopped him. It might have been a pair of large, pleading eyes. Or the deliciously long legs wrapped about the drainpipe. Or even, heaven forbid, the glimpse of something white and lacy that he was certain was a pair of French knickers peeping from beneath her tucked-up dress.

Or maybe it was just simple distaste that any father could conceive of locking up a fully grown woman simply because her idea of what made a good husband did not coincide with his own. Whatever it was, he decided to take Carlisle at his word. Emerald Carlisle, he had been told, was no concern of his. And when the girl let go of the pipe with one hand and urged him to get her father inside the house, with an unmistakable gesture that left her swinging in the most perilous fashion above a well-tended rose border, he didn't hesitate. Patting absently at his jacket pocket, he turned and headed back up the steps. 'I think I left my car keys on your desk, sir.' The 'sir' almost choked him.

Carlisle glared after him. 'Oh, for goodness' sake,' he said, irritably, but followed Brodie back into the house.

* * *

Emerald's heart, already beating an adrenalin-charged tattoo as she eased herself down the drainpipe, had gone into overdrive at the sudden appearance of her father. But the moment her gaze had collided with the dark-eyed stranger standing with him she had known instinctively that she had an ally. He hadn't batted an eyelid at the sight she must have made, had not given her away by so much as a twitch of an eyebrow. Instead he had quite coolly

21

considered his options.

He could have informed her father that he appeared to have an incompetent cat burglar clinging to his drainpipe.

Or he could have ignored the situation, pretended he hadn't seen her and hoped she didn't fall into the roses.

Only a man without a scrap of imagination would have considered either of them. What the dark-eyed stranger had done was offer her the opportunity to escape by creating a diversion.

That kind of swift thinking was so *rare*, she thought. Poor Kit would have dithered and blushed and quite given the game away. He was sweet and wonderfully talented, but not in the least bit decisive, which was why she had to get to him before her father's henchman.

As she searched amongst the lavender and roses for her shoes she felt a moment of regret that she wouldn't be able to stay and thank Dark-eyes for his chivalry. Were they grey? she wondered.

Or brown? Distance and the dusky light had made it impossible to tell.

Unfortunately she didn't have time for politeness, but she was sure he would understand her need to put the maximum distance between herself and her father before he discovered her escape. If only she could find her other shoe!

She spotted it at last, half-buried behind the tall lavender that edged the border, filling the air with sweet scent as she brushed against it. The roses were not so kind, snagging at her bare arms as she reached for her shoe, catching and tangling her hair with their thorns. She didn't have time to worry about it, or take time to extricate herself carefully, and tugged herself free. The rose retaliated by whipping back and catching at her neck with its thorns. She scarcely noticed. All she knew was that she was taking far too long to get away.

But there was no way she could make her escape barefooted. Her feet would be cut to ribbons on the gravel by the time she had sprinted around to the old coach-house where her car had undoubtedly been stowed after her incarceration. She could just hear her father speaking to the chauffeur. 'Miss Emerald has decided to stay for a few days. Put her car away, will you, Saunders?' All perfectly natural. She made a rude noise as she tipped the dirt out of her shoes and slipped her feet into them.

'Maybe you left your keys in the car, Brodie.' Her father's impatient voice carried through the open front door, pinning her back against the wall.

'I might have dropped them in the hall.'

Brodie. The name had a nice, solid ring to it and Brodie, bless the man, was giving her all the time he could, delaying her father, apparently quite unconcerned at the tetchiness in his voice. Not many men were that brave. Unfortunately his valour would be to little avail. There was no cover within a hundred feet of her exposed position, and any second now she was going to be discovered and dragged ignominiously back to the nursery, where she would probably be put on a diet of bread and water. Not that she cared about that. But poor Kit . . .

Of course, she could always throw herself on Brodie's mercy. In fact the thought of flinging herself into his arms had a definite appeal. She hadn't been mistaken about the shoulders, or his height. And his character spoke for itself.

But, no. He had already done more than enough. To demand he choose between her and her father was more than could be expected of any knight errant. But she was hanged if she was going to give in without a fight. She had mere seconds in which to act before the two men appeared on the steps and she was discovered. She didn't waste it, flinging herself at the BMW, praying that it wasn't locked. Her guardian angel must have been listening because the rear door opened at her touch and she dived in, pulling it shut behind her with heartfelt thanks for the superb German engineering that ensured it closed with scarcely a sound.

She didn't know where her knight errant was going, but at least he was going somewhere. Away from her father, away from Lower Honeybourne. She would throw herself on his mercy, and once they reached civilisation it would only take a telephone call to bring any number of gallants racing to her aid. Meanwhile, she tucked herself down behind the front seats and congratulated herself on her luck.

This might not be the most comfortable way to travel but, on reflection, escape this way was far more likely than in her own car. Any attempt to retrieve that would undoubtedly have attracted the attention of her father's chauffeur, who had a flat above the garages, and by the time she'd reached the electronic security gates they would have been firmly closed.

She would, of course, have climbed over them, but she was well aware that walking along a deserted country road as night fell and without a penny to her name was not an entirely sensible course of action.

Brodie, on the other hand, would drive straight through unchallenged, and since he had already connived with her escape he could scarcely turn around and take her back when she popped up. In fact she rather hoped he might be persuaded to take her home. By morning she would be in France with Kit, and then Hollingworth could do his worst.

There was the added bonus that once they were clear of the park she would be able to sit up and thank Brodie for helping her. The thought brought a smile to her lips. She was absolutely sure that she and Brodie were going to be friends.

There was a crunch of shoes, the driver's door was opened and through the gap between the front seats she saw

27

Brodie palm the keys from his pocket before turning to her father.

'It seems they were on the seat all the time,' Emerald heard him say, almost certainly without a trace of a blush. No one who acted with such swift decisiveness would be fazed by such a tiny white lie. 'I must have dropped them.'

Gerald Carlisle snorted, impatient with such incompetence. 'I thought you were supposed to be Hollingworth's bright new man.' His voice betrayed what he thought of bright new men in general and Brodie in particular. And Emerald froze as he added, 'I just hope you're capable of dealing with this situation efficiently. I don't want it bungled. I particularly don't want it all over the newspapers,' he said, with feeling.

'I'll speak to Kit Fairfax,' Brodie promised. 'If it's money he's after it'll just be a question of haggling.'

'Haggle all you want. Whatever it costs will be cheap if it keeps my daughter out of the hands of some idle layabout who's only after her money.'

'And if he's actually in love with the girl?'

Gerald Carlisle made the kind of explosive, disparaging noise Brodie had always assumed to be the colourful invention of nineteenth century novelists. Apparently not.

'Just use whatever methods you have to ensure they don't get married, Brodie. I'm holding you personally responsible.'

Emerald, tucked behind the passenger seat of Tom's car, froze. *Brodie was being sent to deal with Kit?* Where was Hollingworth? She could deal with that pompous old fool with one hand tied behind her back, but suddenly Brodie's treasured decisiveness was not so welcome, and she gave a little shudder of apprehension.

The beauty of her plan had been in its simplicity. She had been convinced that nothing could possibly go wrong. Which just showed how foolish one person could be.

Brodie tossed the folder he was carrying onto the passenger seat and climbed behind the wheel while Emerald made herself as small as she could. Suddenly popping up the moment they were clear of the estate and introducing herself no longer seemed so appealing.

Brodie might be terribly kind to girls who flashed their knickers when they climbed down drainpipes, but she was very much afraid that he wouldn't be anything like as soft-hearted when it came to dealing with fortune-hunters. Or as easy to mislead as the unimaginative Hollingworth.

Which made it imperative she get to darling Kit before Brodie could talk to him, or she had a feeling the poor sweetheart wouldn't know what had hit him.

2

Brodie leaned forward, started the car, then lowered the window. He paused for a moment, taking in the great, sweeping parkland of Carlisle's estate, curling his lip at the privilege it represented, at the man's absolute certainty that money was the solution to every problem. The truth, he had discovered in the course of his legal career, was that money was the cause of most of them. It was certainly the cause of the problem that confronted him now. If Emerald Carlisle had been a penniless working girl she could have married whom she pleased and no one would have given a damn, except to wish them happy.

He dwelt momentarily on the image of the long-limbed girl who, ten minutes ago, had been clinging to the drainpipe, and wondered if Kit Fairfax loved her enough to resist the bribe. He discovered that his feelings were oddly mixed.

Then, as he pulled away from the golden stone frontage of Honeybourne Park, he put the distasteful task ahead of him firmly out of his mind and began to think about a more pressing concern. He hadn't eaten since his secretary had brought him a sandwich at his desk at lunchtime and he was hungry. He had noticed a promising-looking inn in the village, but on reflection decided it might be advisable to put some distance between himself and Carlisle before he stopped. It had been made quite plain that he was expected to get back to London and deal with Fairfax without delay. Somehow he didn't think hunger would be considered an adequate excuse for putting off the evil moment.

Brodie pulled a face. Even if he drove straight back to town it would be too late to do anything useful. The situation was unpleasant enough without the additional farce of hammering on

Fairfax's door in the middle of the night to remind him of his lowly status and demand he forget all about marrying Emerald Carlisle.

Remembering the girl's expressive eyes, her warm mouth that had formed a natural smile, he knew that if the situation were reversed he would tell any legal busybody who came interfering in their relationship to get lost. Forcefully. Somehow, though, he couldn't see Kit Fairfax hitting him. The man had a slightly distracted look, a gentleness about his face, and Tom Brodie knew that whatever happened he was going to feel like a heel. Which was ridiculous. Kit Fairfax had been cast in that role. Maybe he was. The one thing Tom had learned over the years was to keep an open mind.

He shrugged. Whatever. Food was his first priority. Well, perhaps not quite his first priority. He was suddenly aware that he had another and rather more pressing problem. Spotting a lay-by ahead, he slowed and pulled into it.

It hadn't taken Emerald long to realise that travelling undetected all the way to London on the floor of the car was not going to be as easy as she had thought. Within minutes her legs had begun to cramp from the awkwardness of her position, and she was losing the feeling in one of her shoulders. She eased herself slightly and for a moment there was some relief. Then the pain was back, settling itself in her lumbar region like a cat making itself at home in a favoured chair. Nothing was going to shift it while she remained crouched in this awkward position. She pulled a face; she could stand a little pain in the cause of freedom. All she had to do was hold on for a little and hope that Brodie would have to stop for petrol, or even, she thought as her stomach began to remind her just how hungry she was, something to eat. Then she would be able to make her escape.

Even as she shifted the weight back to her shoulder the car began to slow. She held her breath, trying to make out where they were but not daring to raise her head. A pub car park maybe. There certainly weren't enough lights to suggest a garage forecourt. She crossed her fingers and eased her head slowly around to check the other window. Brodie, half-turned in his seat, his face unreadable in the gathering darkness, was watching her cautious manoeuvring. She froze, suddenly knowing exactly how a mouse felt when cornered by a cat. If she closed her eyes and kept very still perhaps he would lose interest, think he had imagined the whole thing. Except that Brodie had a lot more imagination than your average moggie. Far better to brazen it out.

So she gave a little shrug. 'Don't mind me,' she said, with a dismissive little gesture. 'I won't cause you any bother.' Her grin, she knew, was disarming. 'Honest.'

He was not, apparently, disarmed. Maybe he couldn't see it. Whatever, he didn't smile back. 'You'll forgive me if I reserve judgement on that for the moment. In the meantime, since you're not wearing a seatbelt — ' his voice didn't give much away either ' — I'm going to have to insist you join me up here. For your own safety.'

There was something about Brodie that suggested she was safer where she was. Nothing overtly threatening. Just an uneasy feeling that she might have done better taking her chances with the unlit country road. Well, not even the most gallant of knights errant appreciated being taken for a ride. Or vice versa.

'I could sit in the back,' she offered. 'You could pretend I wasn't here. If that would help.' He didn't answer, simply waited for her to obey him. There was something unnerving about that. Her father would have blustered, bullied. Hollingworth would have spoken to her in that maddeningly patronising way of his, treating her like a little girl who had to be cajoled into taking a spoonful of nasty medicine. Brodie was different. A few minutes earlier she had been congratulating herself on that. Maybe she had been too quick in her judgement.

Emerald shrugged. At least he hadn't turned around and taken her straight back to her father. Yet.

She took a certain comfort from the awkwardness of his position in regard to her father. After all, it was because of him that she had managed to escape in the first place. Which didn't answer the question uppermost in her mind. What *did* he propose to do with her? Since Brodie had been engaged to deal with Kit, buy him off, she couldn't expect him to actively aid and abet her runaway marriage.

It took Emerald a few moments to extricate herself from her cramped quarters. She didn't hurry about it, giving herself as much time as possible to decide on a plan of action, slowly stretching each of her cramped limbs in turn even while her mind was whirring into action. By the time she was perched on the rear seat, her elbows propped on the seat in front of her, her chin resting in the palms of her hands, she had decided that there was only one way to handle Brodie. She would have to make him fall just a little bit in love with her. It was something she had always found extremely easy to do and, while she knew she would feel incredibly guilty afterwards, she didn't have time to worry about that right now.

'Hello, Brodie,' she said, with the kind of smile that made the street lighting redundant. 'I'm Emmy Carlisle. But you already know that.' She extended her hand. He took it, held it for just a moment.

'I'm Tom Brodie. How d'you do?' he replied, with just the barest trace of amusement at such formality.

She'd known he'd have a sense of humour. A promising start. 'How d'you do, Tom Brodie? Are you by any chance going to London?'

Her smile was infectious. It was the kind of smile to tempt the unwary, to captivate and charm the jaded sensibilities of a man who had ground his way to the top of his profession with never a moment for simple fun. Innocent of guile and yet oddly seductive, it was the kind of smile that would get a man into all sorts of trouble. It already had, Brodie acknowledged wryly, as with difficulty he resisted the urge to smile right back.

'And if I'm not?'

Emmy Carlisle wasn't in the least put out by this unpromising answer. 'Then I'm afraid you're on the wrong road,' she told him, poised as a duchess at a garden party and apparently not in the least embarrassed at being caught stowing away in his car. 'And it would be just the tiddliest bit of a nuisance. But if you could drop me at the nearest hotel I'm sure someone could be persuaded to come and fetch me.' Her smile never wavered. 'If you could loan me the money for the telephone.'

It was becoming increasingly difficult to keep a straight face. 'Shall we start

with the hotel and take it from there?'
Brodie replied dryly. 'Maybe you can
suggest somewhere. I'm not familiar
with this road, and I was looking for
somewhere to eat.'

'Oh, what a good idea. I am
absolutely starving.' Confident now that
he wasn't going to take her back, she
wriggled through the gap between the
seats, settled herself beside him and
fastened her seatbelt. 'My father locked
me in the nursery, you see, so I went on
hunger strike.'

'Since four o'clock?' It was a guess.
Carlisle had summoned him to Lower
Honeybourne just after four. Apparently he was near the mark because she
pouted. He normally loathed women
who pouted. But it was impossible to
loathe Emmy Carlisle, especially since
she was laughing at herself and inviting
him to join her. 'How fortunate I happened along; you might have expired by
morning.'

'It's quite possible,' she told him, her
earnest tone belied by a flash of

mischief in her eyes. 'I've already missed afternoon tea and dinner. In fact I haven't eaten a thing since lunchtime.'

'I seem to have missed out on the cucumber sandwiches, too. And my own dinner engagement had to be cancelled at the last moment.'

'Oh, I'm sorry,' she said, with feeling. Then, 'Was she very cross?'

He recalled the icy politeness with which his telephone call had been received by the silver-blonde. The lady was not used to being stood up. 'It doesn't matter,' he said. He discovered, rather to his surprise, that it didn't.

'I'm sorry.'

'You should be.'

She gave him a thoughtful look. 'I don't think we should leave it too long before we find somewhere to eat,' she said, 'or our blood-sugar levels will be dangerously depleted. That could be why you're so irritable.'

'Quite possibly.'

She gave him a long look, as if not

41

quite sure how to take that remark. 'You're angry with me for stowing away in your car.'

'No. With myself. I should have locked it.'

'Yes,' she agreed, 'I suppose you should. But I'm very glad you didn't. How did you know I was there?' she asked as they pulled away from the lay-by. 'What gave me away?' He glanced at her. 'I wouldn't want to make the same mistake again,' she pointed out.

'Your scent.' Chanel. He'd saved every penny he had earned on his paper round to buy his mother a bottle for her birthday. He still remembered her face as she had opened the wrapping, seen the tiny white box with its black edging. He'd never been quite sure whether the tear she had blinked back had betrayed pleasure or simply frustration that he had spent so much money on something utterly frivolous. Perhaps it had been a little of both. But she had unstoppered the bottle and dabbed a little of the precious liquid behind her ears so that the room had been filled with that distilled essence of femininity. And then she had smiled and he had known it was all right.

Emerald's scent had been masked initially by the sun-warmed roses of Honeybourne Park, the leather interior of the car, but when he had finally caught a breath of it it had been unmistakable, the aroma of it imprinted on his memory.

'My scent? Oh, Lord, I didn't think of that. I wouldn't be any use as a spy, would I?' She didn't wait for him to answer, but, casually retrieving her stockings from her bra, kicked off her shoes and, stretching out one long leg, began to slowly draw the fine nylon up to her thigh, apparently oblivious of the effect this performance was having on Brodie. Or perhaps she wasn't. He glanced briefly across at her, then kept his eyes firmly fixed on the road ahead.

Emmy, smoothing the stockings into place, continued, 'Actually, I am rather pleased you noticed me, Brodie. I wasn't going to embarrass you by declaring my presence, but I did want to thank you for not saying anything back there.' She looked up and gave him another of those incandescent smiles. 'When I was hanging from the drainpipe,' she added, in case he wasn't sure what she was talking about.

'I should have,' he said, rather hoarsely.

'Oh, no. You were an absolute brick. It's so rare one meets a real knight errant these days.'

'I'm no knight errant,' he warned.

'Don't underestimate yourself. But it's a pity my father asked you to sort out Kit. I was sure he'd get Hollingworth to do the dirty deed.'

'I wasn't his first choice,' he assured her. 'Unfortunately Hollingworth is in Scotland decimating the grouse population, along with choices two, three and four.'

'Bother.'

'I said much the same thing,' he said dryly.

'I'd forgotten the Glorious Twelfth.'

He glanced at her. 'It won't work, you know.'

'Work?'

Innocence personified. 'I may have turned my back when you shinned down the drainpipe, Miss Carlisle, and you've managed to hijack a lift to London, but first thing in the morning I shall carry out your father's instructions.'

'Not first thing in the morning.'

'I can assure you, I'm an early riser.' And this was one job he wanted over and done with.

'If you want to talk to Kit first thing in the morning you're going to have to drive all night. He's in France.'

He threw her a startled glance. 'France?'

'He went last week.'

'Where in France?' Brodie demanded.

'Why don't we pull in here and we can talk about it over dinner?'

He glanced at the cheerful, twenty-four-hour café, scarcely crediting that

45

she was serious. 'You're kidding?'

'No. This place serves breakfast all day and that's my favourite meal.' Then she grinned at him. 'We're not in London, Brodie. It's rather late for the more conventional restaurants in this part of the world. Anyone who arrives much after nine is likely to get seriously scowled at.'

Brodie doubted that anyone had scowled at Emerald Carlisle in a very long time, if ever. Except perhaps her father. He was beginning to have a guilty twinge of sympathy for the man. If he had locked her up it was quite possible that he had good cause. The girl was clearly quite capable of behaving in an entirely irresponsible manner, and, if he was not exactly conspiring with her, there was no doubt he was an accessory to her bolt for freedom. Determined to put a stop to any impression that he was prepared to help her any further, he forced his face into its sternest expression and turned to her.

He was confronted by Emmy Carlisle, her eyes pleading beneath the most fetchingly arched brows, her mouth suddenly uncertain, her curls tousled about her cheeks . . . What colour was her hair? When he had seen her hanging from that wretched drainpipe the twilight had leached away the colour. Suddenly he had to know. He reached up and switched on the light. Red. Not auburn. Not chestnut. Nothing muted or understated, but brilliant coppery curls that glowed around her head like a halo against her shadowy face. What else?

For a moment neither of them spoke. They simply stared at one another. Then they both spoke at once.

'Red. Of course — '

'Grey,' Emmy said. 'I knew they would be.'

There was another moment of silence. Then Brodie said, 'You've scratched your neck.'

'It must have been the rose. When I was looking for my shoes,' she said, lifting her fingers to feel for the damage as Brodie released his seatbelt to reach for the glove compartment and his first-aid kit. There was a moment of confusion as they became entangled and the smooth skin of her arm, ripened to a delicate apricot by the long, hot summer, momentarily entwined with his, a bewitching contrast to the dark grey of his jacket. And as he turned to extricate himself her face was just below his, her eyes shaded by long silky lashes, her lips softly parted over small, very white teeth. There was a split second, an immeasurable moment, when every cell in his body urged him to kiss her. When he knew she was waiting for him to kiss her. And he knew it would have been special.

Too special. To kiss her would be wrong, and somehow he resisted. He hadn't come this far, travelling light-years from his working class roots in the Midlands, to throw everything away on a moment of madness. Besides, the idea that she wanted him to kiss her was ridiculous. She was on the way to her wedding. It might be his job to stop it, but not like that.

'What's grey?' he asked, his voice catching slightly.

'Your eyes.' She opened hers wide. They were hazel, bewitchingly green-flecked, with tiny strands of gold. 'I wondered.'

He turned away quickly, retrieved the first-aid kit from the glove compartment with fingers that were not quite as steady as they might have been and flipped it open. 'Here,' he said, tearing open a small pouch containing an antiseptic wipe and handing it to her. 'You'd better clean that scratch.'

Emmy let her head fall back, exposing her neck. 'Will you do it for me? Please, Brodie? I won't be able to see what I'm doing.'

Idiot. He should have given her the pouch and pointed her in the direction of the café's cloakroom. Instead he turned her chin slightly, aware of the soft warmth of her skin beneath his fingers as he dabbed at the scratch that jagged vividly across her long neck, grateful for the sharp tang of antiseptic blotting out her scent, clearing his head. Roses smelt sweet and their petals were like velvet, but they had thorns, too, he reminded himself. She might be an English rose, but Emerald Carlisle was trouble. With a capital T.

As Brodie dabbed at her neck Emmy drew in a sharp breath, flinched slightly. 'Did that hurt?' he asked.

She had the fleeting impression that he hoped it was hurting like hell. Well, it was, but she wasn't about to admit it. Besides, it proved that he wasn't quite as immune to her charms as his straight face would have her believe.

'It was cold, took my breath away for a moment, that's all.' If she was honest with herself, she had been feeling decidedly breathless ever since Brodie had turned on the light and looked at her with those slatey dark eyes. And a moment ago, when she had been sure that he was going to kiss her, her entire heart had momentarily stopped in its tracks. Now it was trying to make up for lost time.

She wondered what had stopped him. Then she blinked. Was she quite mad? Had she quite forgotten about Kit? Having Brodie fall in love with her was one thing. Encouraging him to make love to her was something else entirely.

'That's fine now,' she said, with determined briskness, raking her fingers through her hair in an attempt to make it look tidy.

Brodie considered offering her his comb, but decided he rather liked her hair the way it was. But he couldn't resist the smallest dig. 'Don't you have a comb secreted somewhere about your person?' he asked, his gaze lingering momentarily on the point where the scooped neck of her dress dipped down over her breasts. 'How disappointing.'

This veiled reference to the way she had stored her stockings, the display she had made of herself putting them on — a suggestion that he knew exactly what she had been up to — brought colour flooding to Emmy's cheeks. She could hardly believe it. A blush. It was impossible. She hadn't blushed since she was six years old. 'I have,' she fibbed. 'But I'm too modest to retrieve it.'

'Liar.'

'Are you suggesting that I'm not modest, or that I haven't got a comb, Brodie?'

'Both.'

Emmy regarded Tom Brodie thoughtfully. A minute earlier he had been eating out of her hand and she had been sure that everything was going to be all right. Suddenly she wasn't so sure. It would be a mistake to underestimate him. She opened the car door. 'Come on. I'm starving.'

The cheerful comfort food was quickly produced by a motherly waitress wearing a badge that invited them to call her Betty and promised that she would do everything she could to make their day a happy one.

Emmy tucked into a pile of bacon and scrambled eggs. Brodie, feeling overdressed in the informal atmosphere of the café took off his jacket and hung it over the back of his chair, loosened his tie, then attacked his own more conventional lamb cutlet with equal enthusiasm.

'I'm sorry if I've caused you a lot of bother, Brodie,' Emmy said when she had finished. She propped her elbows on the table and rested her chin on her hands so that her long, slender fingers formed a frame for her face; her nose, he decided, had just the right number of tiny pale freckles. As if it had been lightly dusted with gold. 'But I really couldn't allow Fa to get away with locking me up in the nursery like a naughty child, could I?'

Freckles? Gold dust? Brodie made a serious effort to pull himself together. 'He does appear to have left it rather late. Maybe if he had put you over his knee when you were little you wouldn't be such a pain in the backside now.'

She pulled a face. 'I'm twenty-three next month. That's old enough to make decisions for myself. Wouldn't you say?' she persisted, when he was slow to reply.

'Under normal circumstances,' he said, carefully. 'Unfortunately your money makes things anything but normal.'

'My money,' she said, with disgust. 'Everything comes back to that. It's positively indecent that any one person should have so much. I wanted to give it away the minute I reached twenty-one, but Hollingworth wouldn't hear of it.'

Brodie might agree with the sentiment but he knew better than to say so. Gerald Carlisle's anxiety about his daughter appeared to be well founded. 'Maybe Mr Hollingworth thinks you'd regret it. Later,' he offered, noncommittally.

'Hollingworth.' She said the name

with disgust. 'He treats me like a two-year-old. He actually lectures me if I spend more than my allowance.'

'Does he?'

'It's *my* money,' she declared. 'You'd think I could do what I wanted with it.'

That rather depended on what she wanted to do with it. Brodie poured a second cup of coffee. Anything rather than meet those eyes — all flashing indignation, he had no doubt. Anything rather than dwell on the thought of James Hollingworth reading Emmy Carlisle the riot act over a spending spree. He was having enough trouble keeping his face straight as it was.

'He's just doing his job.'

'Will you do yours with the same dedication?'

He finally gathered himself sufficiently to meet her gaze. 'If you mean will I try and persuade Kit Fairfax that marrying you is not in his best interests, I'm afraid the answer is yes.'

'There isn't anything I can do to dissuade you?'

'Why would you want to? If he loves you nothing I say will have the power to change his mind.' Emmy didn't bother to answer. Why on earth had Hollingworth had to go away *this* week? The man might be an old stick-in-the-mud, but he was two-dimensional in his thinking and absolutely predictable. It would never occur to him to doubt her sincerity, but after only a few minutes in Brodie's company she sensed that he was quite different. She simply had to get to Kit before he did. 'Tell me about Fairfax,' Brodie invited.

Emmy regarded him suspiciously. 'What do you want to know?'

'How did you meet him?'

'He came into Aston's for a valuation.'

'The auction house?'

'Mmm. I work there.'

It hadn't occurred to Brodie that Emerald Carlisle might actually have a job. 'Was he buying, or selling?'

'The lease on his studio runs out soon.' Too late she saw the trap. 'It's not easy getting a loan when you're an artist,' she said, defensively.

'That depends on how successful you are.'

'He's very talented. He will be successful. But at the moment . . . ' She shrugged.

'I can see that it might be difficult.' He could also see why he might be keen to latch onto a gullible heiress. 'And was it love at first sight?'

There was the merest hesitation before she said, 'What else?'

Brodie glanced at the modest engagement ring she was wearing. It was oddly touching. 'And now he's in France waiting for you to join him. Are you going to tell me where?'

She gave a little sigh. 'I've already told you far too much.'

He wasn't convinced by the sigh, but he didn't press her for an answer. Instead he finished his coffee and excused himself. He had noticed a pay-phone in the lobby on the way in. There was a telephone in the car, but he would prefer that Emmy didn't know he was making a call.

He punched in the number. 'Mark Reed Investigations.' The response was laconic.

'Mark, it's Tom Brodie. I understand you've been investigating Kit Fairfax for Gerald Carlisle.'

'What if I have?'

'I've been told he's in France. Would you have any idea where?'

'Not a clue. I was just asked to find out anything I could about his background when Miss Carlisle started to take an interest in him.'

'You didn't turn up any French connection? Has he got friends there for instance? Someone he might be staying with for a while? Somewhere he might be waiting for her to join him?'

'Not that I know of. He certainly hasn't got the money to keep a place of his own.' There was a momentary pause. 'You could try looking at it from the opposite direction. I imagine Miss Carlisle has any number of friends with converted farmhouses in the Dordogne or Provence where they might get together.'

Brodie stifled a groan. 'Just see what you can dig up, will you? Maybe he left a number with a neighbour in case of emergencies.'

'Maybe, although I wouldn't have put him down as the kind of man to worry much about emergencies. He's a bit laid back.'

'Do what you can.' He momentarily considered calling Gerald Carlisle. It didn't take much imagination to guess the state the man was in. He decided against it. Emerald Carlisle, he had been told, was not his problem. Well, once he had dropped her off at her apartment, she wouldn't be.

When he returned to their table, Emmy had gone to powder her nose. He settled the bill and glanced at his watch, calculating the length of time it would take them to get to London, mentally rescheduling his appointments for the next couple of days while he tracked down Kit Fairfax.

'Everything all right, sir?' Betty was clearing their table.

'Yes, fine, thank you. At least . . . ' He glanced at his watch again. Emmy was taking an awfully long time to powder her nose . . . considering she didn't have any powder to start with. He felt a sudden lurch of alarm. 'Would you mind checking the ladies' cloakroom for me, Betty? I'm just a little concerned about my companion.'

'No problem.' She was back in thirty seconds, her calm exterior seriously ruffled. 'The young lady isn't in the cloakroom, sir. But she left you a message. You'd better come and see for yourself.'

Emmy had written on the long mirror, using green liquid soap. 'Thanks, Galahad. I'll send you an invitation to the wedding.' She'd signed her name with a flourish and added a cross for good measure.

The window was open, swinging slightly in the warm breeze and he didn't need to look out into the car park to know that his car was missing; he knew exactly what she'd done. A quick check of his jacket confirmed that while he was on the telephone she'd helped herself to his car keys, then legged it through the toilet window.

And, if she drove with the same dash that she did everything else, she was probably miles away by now. His only hope was that she would be stopped for speeding. He considered calling the local police to report his car had been stolen. A night in jail would certainly slow Miss Carlisle down, he thought grimly.

A nice thought, but he discarded it immediately. It was his responsibility to keep Emerald out of the papers, not hand them a story. Gerald Carlisle would, quite rightly, have a fit if his daughter was hauled before the local magistrate for stealing his solicitor's car, and the press would have a field day. And when Carlisle had finished having a fit about that, he'd want to know exactly what his daughter was doing in Brodie's car in the first place.

He couldn't believe he had been so careless. No, he corrected himself, not careless. Far worse than careless. Just plain stupid. He'd already seen irrefutable evidence of Emerald's determination to get her own way. Good grief, she'd already shinned down a fifty-foot drainpipe without turning so much as a hair — a small ground-floor window wasn't going to cause her any problem.

He wanted to swear, loudly and at length, but he didn't. He'd already over-indulged on idiocy for one day. Emerald Carlisle had batted her long silky eyelashes at him from that drainpipe and he had been putty in her hands ever since.

Nor was there time to waste in berating himself for getting himself into such a jam, telling himself that he should have ignored those pleading eyes and ratted on her the moment he'd spotted her behind Gerald Carlisle's back. What he had to do, without delay, was to get the genie back in the bottle. But first he had to catch the genie.

'Betty,' he said, turning to the waitress, 'I need a car. Right now. So tell me, is that badge you're wearing just so much window dressing? Or are you about to make my day a happy one?'

3

Emerald could not believe her luck. Talk about out of the frying pan and into the fire.

She'd noticed the telephone in the entrance lobby when they'd arrived and had decided to put out a reverse-charge call for help the moment the opportunity presented itself. Just in case Brodie decided that it was in his best interests to return her to her father.

She waited until he went to the washroom, and the minute he was out of sight she made for the phone. Except he didn't go to the washroom. He was using the telephone himself. Fortunately he had his back to her and didn't notice her abrupt about-turn.

She had to admit that she was disappointed in him. For a moment there she had hoped he might just be something *really* special. A Galahad with just enough of Lancelot to add a little excitement. He had come so close to kissing her. She felt a tiny clench of disappointment in her midriff as she wondered what had stopped him. The thought of her father at their heels? No, she decided, with a certain satisfaction, at that moment the last thing on his mind had been her father. She should have made it impossible for him to resist . . .

She swallowed the thought down, hard. That wouldn't help right now; this wasn't the moment for self-indulgence.

She had escaped once; she could do it again. Her gaze alighted on the jacket slung across the back of Brodie's recently vacated seat and she wondered — but not for long. She didn't have time to waste wondering. It was time for action and she acted, dipping her hand into the pocket. Her fingers tightened around the keys to the BMW. *Yes!* She glanced towards the lobby. Did she dare take them? Brodie would be livid. Off-the-scale angry.

The thought sent a little frisson of alarm tingling up her backbone. If he caught up with her . . . *when* he caught up with her . . . She quelled it. This was not the moment for faint heart. Or an attack of conscience.

Right now he was telephoning her father, she reminded herself severely. Telling him where she was.

Yet even as she eased herself through the tiny washroom window she was prepared to give him the benefit of the doubt. She was sure that he didn't *mean* to rat on her; he just wanted to reassure her father that she was safe. It was what any knight errant would do, after all. But she knew her father a whole lot better than Brodie did. And she wasn't sure that a father who treated his grown-up daughter like a five-year-old deserved to have peace of mind. At least, not one who locked her in the rotten nursery.

The real problem was that Brodie was working for her father. He might sympathise, but he'd done just about as much as she could expect. More than anyone could expect. She giggled. He hadn't invited her along for the ride after all, although she had to admit she had enjoyed it while it had lasted.

And she hadn't finished with Brodie. Not by a long chalk. But he was going to need careful handling if he wasn't going to mess up her plans.

Emmy reached the motorway and regretfully put all thoughts regarding the handling of Brodie on hold as she moved out into the fast lane to overtake a truck. She'd gained herself a little time, but it wouldn't take Brodie long to smell the proverbial rodent. She very much doubted that he was still sitting patiently in the café, waiting for her to emerge from the ladies' loo. It might take him some time to organise alternative transport. But not that much time. He wasn't the kind of man to sit on his backside and wait for fate to lend a helping hand; he was a man of action. And, with that thought to lend urgency to her mission, she put her foot down and concentrated on getting to London as quickly as she could.

* * *

Betty's badge had been anything but an idle boast.

'Is it,' she had asked, putting a sympathetic hand on Brodie's arm, 'an affair of the heart?'

'Yes. It's an affair of the heart,' Brodie assured her with considerable feeling.

'You're in love with her?'

That was trickier, and he couldn't bring himself to actually lie to the woman. 'She's going to marry someone else, unless I can stop her,' he said, obliquely.

'Oh, no. That will never do. Your auras were quite definitely linked.'

Brodie wasn't sure that was something to be entirely happy about, but Betty clearly expected some response. 'Linked?' he repeated, trying to sound happy.

'There was no mistaking it. You were made for each other.' He stifled his impatience. He needed transport — what he'd got was a mystic with a romantic streak a mile wide. 'Now, you just wait here, dear.' She patted his arm absently. 'I'll be right back.' For one awful moment he had thought she was going to fetch a pack of tarot cards, but Betty had something far more practical in mind, and when she returned it was to press her car keys into his hand. 'Go after her. You can let me have the car back when you like.'

Brodie gave her the money for a taxi home at the end of her shift, but he still felt guilty about taking advantage of her good nature. The poor woman was probably chewing her fingernails down to the quick right now as the romantic auras evaporated and cold reality asserted itself. She'd be wondering if she'd ever see her precious little car again, wondering what her insurance company's reaction would be when she tried to explain what she'd done in the event that it disappeared for good. Worst of all, she would have to face her husband's ridicule for allowing herself to be taken in by a perfect stranger.

He'd just have to make sure he made her day a really happy one when the car was returned. He'd leave instructions for his secretary to have it valeted first, and make sure the tank was filled with petrol, with a cheque in the glove compartment to cover the inconvenience. And a hand-tied bouquet of roses delivered to the café along with a bottle of something warming for her husband. Sorting out Betty was a piece of cake compared to Emerald Carlisle. The smile abruptly left his face. That young woman was another matter entirely.

He was making good time, but he knew he didn't have a hope of catching her. He had called Mark Reed again before he'd left the café to ensure that there would be someone to keep an eye on her when she arrived home. And, more embarrassingly, to get her address. The file her father had given him was still in the car. He'd thrown it on the back seat when she had come up to sit beside him, and he hoped she didn't notice it, or, if she did, would have the good manners not to look at it. And he was praying that she didn't drive straight down to Dover and onto the first ferry that happened to be sailing.

It seemed unlikely. He could easily have reported the car stolen. She must know that he would be angry enough, but she was also bright enough to know that was the last thing he would want to do. Would she risk it?

Or would she go home for a change of clothes? All she had with her were the clothes on her back, and there wasn't a woman in the world — not even Emerald Carlisle — who would run away to get married without so much as a lipstick to her name.

And then certainty brought a grim little smile to the hard line of his mouth. Just the clothes on her back. A dress, to be more precise. An elegant, sleeveless creation in French blue linen that skimmed her figure and flared gently over her hips. A dress for a lady, with nothing as practical as pockets to spoil the line. She had no money, no passport, no driving licence. She had to go home; she had no choice. And he'd be right behind her.

She had, he judged, about twenty minutes' start on him, but while she had a much faster car it wouldn't give her that much of an edge since, under the circumstances, she wouldn't risk getting stopped by the police for speeding. Maybe. He hoped she was seriously worried by the prospect, but somehow he doubted it. He didn't think that worrying was something Emerald Carlisle had had a lot of practice in.

Still, twenty minutes was a lot of time to make up, and she wouldn't waste too much time packing because she had to assume her father had missed her by now and was moving heaven and earth to find her. He just hoped the man hadn't worked out how his daughter had managed to disappear so completely.

*   *   *

Emerald pulled into her parking space outside her apartment block. 'New car, Miss Carlisle?' the porter asked as he opened the door for her.

She pulled a face. Nothing would induce her to change her bright red MG, not even Brodie's whisper-smooth monster. 'It's not quite my style, Gary,' she said, handing him the keys. 'It belongs to a friend. Keep an eye on it, will you? His name's Brodie, and he'll be along to collect it later.' And he wouldn't be in a good mood. 'Will you give him the keys and tell him thank you for me?'

'Of course, Miss Carlisle.'

'And I need a taxi in about fifteen minutes.' Everything was packed, ready. Passport, traveller's cheques. She just needed time to shower and change. 'I'll be away for a week or so. Will you cancel the papers and milk for me?'

'I'll see to it, Miss Carlisle. Are you going somewhere nice?'

'France,' she said, after a moment's consideration, then, because she didn't want to give Brodie more trouble than absolutely necessary, she added, 'The South of France.' Then she smiled. 'I'll send you a postcard.'

'I'll look forward to it. Give me a buzz when you want me to collect your bag.'

She did. But when she opened the door it wasn't the porter standing in the hall, it was Brodie.

'Carry your bag, lady?' he asked. He was smiling, but it wasn't a smile that suggested good humour.

She opened her mouth to ask how on earth he'd caught up with her so quickly. Then, realising that it didn't matter, she closed it again, backing into her apartment as Brodie picked up her bag and advanced on her, shutting the door behind him with a finality that made the tiny hairs on the back of her neck stand on end.

'I didn't expect to see you again quite so soon,' she said.

'No,' he said, dryly. 'But you must have expected I'd turn up eventually. Or did you hope I wouldn't make it until the wedding?'

'How on earth did you do it? Did you steal a car?'

'Like you, Emmy? No. A kind lady lent me hers because your aura was linked with mine. She didn't want to see you make a mistake.'

'What?' He didn't enlighten her. 'I didn't steal your car, Brodie. I had no intention of depriving you of it permanently.'

'Is that right? Maybe I should call the police now and leave you to argue the point of law with a magistrate.'

'You wouldn't.' Her challenge had the confidence of experience. 'My father would . . . would . . . '

'Would what? Get Hollingworth to

fire me? I'm a partner, Emmy. Hollingworth couldn't afford it. Or the publicity. But you know your father better than I do. Would you like to try?'

Emerald hated to be bested by anyone, but it occurred to her that a display of temper would not be in her best interests right now. So she smiled. 'Come on, Brodie. You've won. Don't be sore. Have a drink. You could probably do with one.'

'I probably could,' he agreed. 'But not right now.'

'Coffee, then?' She headed towards the kitchen.

She wanted him to relax, Brodie thought. She hadn't given up. Everything she really needed was in the bag slung over her shoulder. Clothes could be bought anywhere.

The minute he sat down in one of her comfortable armchairs, she'd abandon her luggage and tiptoe out of the front door. While he found himself in sympathy with her determination, he really couldn't allow her to get away with it again. 'Kit Fairfax's address will do just fine to be going on with,' Brodie replied.

She stopped, turned in the doorway, that pleading look back in her eyes. It touched something in him, tugging at some almost forgotten sweetness from that time before he had become utterly single-minded, focused on success to the exclusion of everything else, and for a moment he wavered. But only for a moment. That was the look which had got him into this situation in the first place, while he'd been still irritated by Gerald Carlisle's 'other ranks' attitude. He told himself that it was a look she practised in front of the mirror, like the one that had nearly made him lose his head completely and kiss her.

'I'm sorry to spoil your plans, but I don't have time to wait for the formal invitation. I have to talk to Fairfax now, Emmy.'

'Talk him out of marrying me, you mean. It won't work.'

'Won't it?' For a moment, for her

sake, he wanted to believe her. Then common sense kicked in. 'If you believed that, Emmy, you wouldn't care whether I talked to him or not. If he loves you nothing I can offer him will change his mind.'

'My father believes that everyone has a price.'

'And you agree with him? Well, maybe Fairfax will prove him wrong.' There was a part of Brodie that would like Fairfax to prove Gerald Carlisle wrong. But there was another, more insistent part of him that was determined she wouldn't marry the man. As he glanced around at the exquisitely furnished sitting room, the delicate water-colours on the wall, the tiny antique treasures in a glass-topped display cabinet, he thought that Fairfax would be mad to settle for as little as a hundred thousand pounds.

He turned back to face her. 'You know, Emmy, if you'd wanted a speedy wedding you'd have done a whole lot better to get a licence from a registrar here in London. You could have been married in three days before anyone knew a thing about it.'

'I wanted a proper wedding,' she said, defiantly. 'In the village church with everyone there. Including my father.'

'Really?' Why didn't he believe that? Because Emerald Carlisle hadn't done anything to date to suggest she was that conventional? Even unconventional girls wanted a white wedding. 'Why didn't you take Kit with you to meet your father?'

She shifted her shoulders awkwardly. 'I thought it would be better if I paved the way first. And Kit wanted to paint,' she said. He noted the slightly defensive tone in her voice, stored it away for consideration at leisure.

'And that was more important than making a good impression on his future father-in-law?' This time she didn't answer. 'You'll have to live in France for a month before you can marry, you know.'

'A whole month? I didn't know that.'

'And provide a stack of documents, all translated into French.'

'Don't go all lawyerish on me, Brodie. We'll sort it out.'

'Eventually. I'll find him before then, so you might as well tell me where he is.'

'And if I don't?'

'If you don't I'll have to take you back to Honeybourne Park, where I'm confident your father will keep a very close eye on you until I've run him to earth. Of course, your father might very well turn up here any minute and save me the bother.'

'I'll tell him you helped me escape.'

'I'll tell him you stowed away in my car and stole it when I stopped for petrol.'

'You wouldn't! That's a downright lie.'

Brodie's grin was slow and tormenting. 'I know. But who do you think he'd believe?' She glared at him. 'You must see that I couldn't possibly take the responsibility of leaving you to run loose . . . ' He waited a moment, then raised his hand in a gesture of resignation when she didn't volunteer her lover's whereabouts. 'No? Well, as you said, France is a very big place. It might take some time, but I'm sure you'll be comfortable at home, locked in the nursery.'

Emmy made a very rude noise. Brodie's arrival had thrown her momentarily, but it needn't, after all, be that much of a problem. She wanted him to find Kit, but not until after she had talked to him first. 'I've had an idea,' she said. 'I won't tell you where Kit is. But I'll take you to him.' Brodie's laugh had a hollow ring to it. 'No, honestly — ' she began.

'Honestly? As in 'I won't cause you any bother, honest' honestly?'

She had the grace to blush. That was twice in one day; Brodie was becoming a serious problem. 'I'm sorry about taking your car, truly. But you can't blame me. When I saw you on the telephone I knew you were telling my father where I was — '

'It's just as well I wasn't, or we'd both be in trouble.'

'Oh.' He waited. 'You weren't calling my father?'

'It didn't seem such a good idea at the time. I can assure you I won't be so soft again.'

'Who were you ringing, then?' She was curious.

'Someone I hoped might have a line on where Fairfax has gone to earth.'

'You mean that odious little man that my father employs to investigate any man who looks at me twice?' He didn't confirm or deny it. But she thought she saw a touch of compassion in those dark eyes. And he hadn't told. The man might have a disconcerting ability to make her blush but he was still a treasure, Emmy decided. One well worth collecting. 'And did he?' she asked. 'Have a line on Kit?'

'No, but fortunately your hall porter was not aware that your destination was a secret. The South of France narrows it down just a little.'

Emerald had to admit she had been careless. She had intended the porter to pass on the information — that was why she had given it to him — but she'd thought she would be well on her way to join Kit when he did. 'You didn't intend to search the *whole* of France, then?' she said.

'I'll have my work cut out, but I'm sure you'll be comfortable at Honeybourne Park while I'm making my enquiries. Can I use your telephone?' Brodie's face broadened into an engaging, slightly lopsided grin that made Emmy's heart give a strange little lurch. What was it about the man? The fact that he refused to be twisted around her little finger? That alone was a challenge. She had never been able to resist a challenge, and she promised herself that she'd bring Brodie to heel in her own good time. But not yet. It was more important to convince him that she was genuine.

'I'll behave, Brodie. I know you've got to do your job, no matter how distasteful it is. I'll take you to Kit and you can put your offer to him. All I ask in return is your promise that if he turns you down that will be an end of it.' That sounded reasonable, didn't it?

'I'd rather you just gave me his address,' Brodie said, unwilling to make any promise he might not be able to keep. 'Or perhaps you think he won't be able to resist your father's money without you there to put a bit of backbone in him?'

Emerald crossed her fingers behind her back. 'I have total confidence in Kit. I just want to be there to see fair play.' She gave a little shrug. 'It will take for ever to find him without my help,' she assured him, her smile seraphic. 'Just how much time can a busy man like you spare?'

Not long, Brodie thought irritably. It had been a straightforward enough matter to deal with Kit Fairfax in London, no matter how distasteful he found it. A few hours at the most. Finding the man in France was something else.

While he didn't trust Emmy further than he could throw her, he knew that he had little choice but to go along with her suggestion. 'All right,' he said. 'You take me to him. I'll talk to him.' And if Fairfax was unexpectedly staunch to his love they still wouldn't be able to marry for a month. Plenty of time for Gerald Carlisle to think of something else. Or maybe even get used to the idea.

Emerald, knowing she had scored the winning point, held out the softly draped slub-silk of her trousers and sketched a little curtsey. 'I'm glad that's settled.' She picked up her bag and handed it to him. 'Shall we go?'

'Go?'

'I'm going to rent a car and drive down to Dover.' She grinned. 'Although now you're here I suppose we could take your car.'

'I've been working since seven this

morning, Emmy. Driving all night is not an option.'

'I can drive,' she pointed out. 'You can sleep.'

He would certainly give her ten out of ten for effort. She never gave up. 'Forgive me if I decline the opportunity to be abandoned in the nearest lay-by.'

'I wouldn't — '

'Of course you would.' He didn't add that he wouldn't blame her. She didn't need any encouragement. 'And I don't have two days to spare to drive south.' Or another two to drive back. 'We'll fly to Marseilles in the morning and I'll hire a left-hand-drive car at the airport.'

'You're a whole lot more than a pair of broad shoulders, Brodie,' she said, with reluctant admiration. He should have been surprised she'd even noticed what he looked like. After all, she was supposed to be head over heels in love with Fairfax. So why wasn't he? He filed the thought away, along with all the other oddities about this business, at the back of his mind. This wasn't the moment to be sidetracked by blatant flattery. 'But there's a problem.'

He stared at her for a moment. 'Go on, surprise me,' he prompted.

'I don't fly.'

'I wasn't expecting you to sprout wings,' he remarked. 'We'll use a regular aircraft, with engines and everything.'

'No, Brodie, I don't fly, even with the aid of engines.'

'Don't or won't?' he asked, suspiciously.

'Both. It's a phobia. The minute they close the aircraft door I have hysterics.'

'I don't believe you.'

Emmy smiled at him. 'Would you like to risk it?'

Brodie regarded her with something close to loathing. He might not believe her, but he didn't underestimate her. He suspected that Emerald Carlisle was perfectly capable of throwing a fit of hysterics that could bring Heathrow to a standstill if she put her mind to it. 'It isn't a problem. We'll take the train.'

'Oh.'

'You're not frightened of trains too, are you?' he asked.

She was tempted. There was, after all, that great big tunnel . . . And it would have been so much easier to get away from Brodie in a car. But she knew when to give in gracefully. 'No,' she said, demurely. 'I love trains.' Trains made stops.

'Good. That only leaves one thing to be decided.' Emmy raised one of those beautifully arched brows of hers. Something else she practised; he'd bank on it. 'Are we going to spend the night here, or at my place?' And, before she could object, 'I'm not taking my eyes off you until we're safely on the train.'

As Emmy opened her mouth to tell him what he could do with his cheek, the telephone began to ring. She threw it a startled glance. 'Oh, Lord that'll be my father,' she said, making no move to answer it.

'Perhaps you should answer it and put his mind at rest. He must be worried about you.'

Emmy pushed her hair back from her face. 'He's worried, you can count on it. But only about money.'

She saw Brodie's brows dip in surprise. 'That's a little harsh, surely? He's just got your best interests at heart.'

'Has he?' The telephone abruptly ceased ringing, and for a moment they both stared at it. 'I wonder if that's the first time he's rung,' Emmy said uneasily.

'Probably not,' Brodie ventured. 'I worked out that you'd have to come here to collect your passport and money, and at least a change of clothes. He's quite capable of making the same calculation. Does it matter?'

'Yes.' Brodie raised a querying brow. 'The answering machine was on,' she explained. 'I checked my messages when I came in and there were a couple of hang-ups that might have been him. I must have forgotten to reset it, so now he'll know I'm home.'

'You're not having a terribly good day.'

She glanced at him, remembering the moment their eyes had met above her father's head. Remembering that moment in the car when he had come so close to kissing her. 'It hasn't all been bad.'

'No?' He clearly wasn't convinced. 'Whatever. It's time to choose the lesser of two evils, Emmy. We can wait here until your father arrives. Or you can come with me.'

For a moment she stared at him. 'No contest. Let's go.' And there was still the taxi waiting downstairs.

She picked up her bag and headed for the door. He hooked his fingers in her belt and brought her to an outraged halt. 'I think I'd be happier if you handed over your passport,' he said.

She pulled a face. 'You're no fun, Brodie. You think of everything.'

'Amusing you was not part of the brief. And if I thought of everything you wouldn't have run off with my car.'

'For all the good it did me. You're just too smart for me.'

He wasn't taken in by her flattery. 'I thought you were going to behave.'

'I am,' she declared.

'Then you won't need your passport, will you?' He wasn't to be distracted, she realised as he stood there, one hand grasping her waistband, the other outstretched, demanding obedience. 'Maybe it would help if I told you that I sent your taxi away?' Emerald capitulated with a shrug of resignation, retrieving her passport from her shoulder bag and handing it over with a grudging smile.

Let him think he'd won some major victory. Once they were in France she wouldn't need her passport. And he couldn't keep his eyes on her *all* the time, could he?

Brodie smiled right back. He had her for the moment, but he was under no illusions. Once they were in France he would have to keep a very close eye on Emmy Carlisle. Fortunately, that wouldn't be a hardship.

* * *

Brodie's flat was not in the same class as Emmy's. He lived in a converted warehouse loft, on the wrong bank of the Thames to be fashionable, that he'd bought at the bottom of the slump when the developer had been glad to be rid of it at any price.

It didn't have a hall porter to take messages and run errands, or a carpeted lift panelled in some rare tropical hardwood. In fact it was served by a vast goods lift that would have taken Brodie's BMW without flinching.

In its favour it had huge open spaces with high ceilings and acres of polished wood floors that gleamed with a dull richness, the perfect setting for the tribal rugs, radiating with almost barbaric colour, that broke up the huge floor area. The furniture, what there was of it, was old and comfortable.

But the white-painted brick walls provided the perfect backdrop for a stunning collection of paintings, the work of talented students, bought before they became unaffordable for a man who worked for his living.

Emmy stood in the centre of the living area and turned slowly around, absorbing every detail. 'I love this,' she said, at last. 'You've got a good eye for a picture. Can I look around?'

'Help yourself. But, I warn you, I've deadlocked the front door and I'm taking the key into the shower with me.'

She swivelled round. 'Really?' Her gaze travelled swiftly over his body. 'I'd be interested to know where you plan to keep it.'

'In the soap dish?' he offered.

'Don't be boring, Brodie. I'm not going to run for it. I promised.'

'So you did.' And butter wouldn't melt in her mouth, he thought. 'While you're looking around the kitchen do feel free to make some tea.'

'Do you really want tea? Or is that just your way of keeping me out of mischief?'

'I have more confidence in your

ability to make mischief than that,' he said cynically. He didn't wait for her retort. He was sure she had one, but he wasn't in the mood to hear it. He was tired and suddenly rather irritable. He was certainly in no mood to play nursemaid to a wilful young woman who was set on getting her own way, even if she lived to rue the day. On top of which he was going to have to surrender his bed. He glanced at the low, wide bed. It was plenty big enough for two. The thought rose unbidden in his head, tormenting him with images of a pair of long, elegant legs, bright, laughing eyes and a mouth that would tempt a saint. He quashed it mercilessly.

He stepped out of his suit and hung it carefully in a walk-in wardrobe full of expensive clothes. There had been a time when one suit had been all he could afford. Old habits died hard.

Perhaps he should have made the effort to find himself an heiress with a father who would rather pay out a fortune than see his daughter married to the son of a miner. With his luck, he chided himself, the father would have called his bluff. And there were very few heiresses who looked like Emerald Carlisle.

He stripped off the rest of his clothes, flicked on the shower and stood for a few moments beneath the hot, reviving needles of water, and while he soaped himself he considered what other tricks Miss Carlisle might have up her sleeve.

She could protest that she was going to 'behave', flash those big innocent eyes and say 'honestly' until the cows came home, but he didn't believe it. Her father had said she was a handful, and Brodie had to admit that the man knew what he was talking about. But going along with Emmy's plan was still the quickest way of getting to Fairfax. Provided she didn't manage to give him the slip.

He wasn't stupid. He knew that it wouldn't be difficult for her to get away from him once they were in France.

She had already demonstrated a reckless daring, a facility for thinking on her feet, the kind of spirit that you would cheer from the sidelines if you weren't the poor sucker being made to look a fool.

He might have learned his lesson regarding car keys, but he knew he wouldn't be able to keep her in sight twenty-four hours a day. However, since the only alternative would be to take her back to her father and own up, he would certainly have to try. A small crease appeared in one corner of his mouth at the thought.

He considered her mop of tousled red hair and a pair of the most bewitching green-gold eyes that he had ever encountered and vowed to make it a priority. About one thing he was in total agreement with Gerald Carlisle. There was no way he was about to let her marry some layabout who called himself an artist and had his eye on her money.

He reached for a towel and wrapped

it about him, but as he walked into the bedroom the telephone at the side of the bed gave the faintest ting. It hadn't taken Emerald long to make herself at home. She was calling someone from the kitchen phone.

He reached for the receiver, lifted it carefully from the cradle and held it to his ear. He was rewarded with the low purr of the dialling tone. Correction. She *had* been calling someone. Fairfax? Or someone else? Only the telephone in the kitchen could give him the answer to that one.

4

Emmy was excessively pleased with herself. To have found Kit in the local café was too much to hope. But the *patron* had taken a message for him, promised to pass it along as soon as he saw him. At least she hoped that was what he'd said. She wished she had paid more attention to French at school.

But in a day that had alternated between exhilarating ups and frustrating downs, the ups had, in the end, come out marginally ahead. And this time Brodie hadn't caught her. That alone was almost enough to put the smile on her face. The kettle boiled, she poured the water on the tea and, picking up the teapot, turned to put it on the tray.

Brodie was standing in the doorway watching her. There was nothing in his expression to indicate how long he had been there. It took every ounce of self-control not to cast a guilty look in the direction of the telephone. Every ounce of self-control to stop her wrist from shaking. And it wasn't just a nervous reaction to coming so close to getting caught once again. Brodie, stripped of the civilising uniform of his business clothes, was a thoroughly dangerous-looking male.

He had discarded his formal suit, the crisp white shirt, regulation dark silk tie and polished shoes for a track-suit bottom worn thin with use and an equally worn T-shirt that hung loosely about his torso. The tendons on his upper arms stood out in relief, as did the veins on his forearms. Deeply tanned forearms. It wasn't sun-bed colour, and his outfit was only thin from being put vigorously to the purpose for which it was intended. His feet — long and beautifully shaped feet — were bare. Which was why she hadn't heard him coming.

It occurred to Emmy that Brodie was wearing this rather unlikely outfit for her benefit. Not the kind of man to wear pyjamas — she suspected any overnight guest wouldn't usually be worried about such niceties — this had been the best he had been able to come up with on short notice. 'Milk, sugar?' she asked as her wrist finally succumbed to the shakes and she put the pot down rather suddenly.

Brodie raked his hand through hair still wet from the shower. He hadn't expected her to do what he'd asked. It wasn't in character. Maybe Emmy thought if she was obviously busy he wouldn't wonder what else she might have been up to while he'd been in the shower. 'Just milk. Thanks. Aren't you having a cup?'

'Not before going to bed.'

'Oh, well, the bedroom is all yours,' he said. 'Come on, I'll show you.'

'Bedroom?' she enquired, looking in at the austere white room, the enormous bed covered by a plain black quilt. 'Singular? Haven't you got a spare room?'

'Not with a bed in it. The need hasn't arisen in the past.'

That she could believe. 'But where will you sleep?'

He shrugged. 'I'll be fine on the sofa.'

'Really?' She looked doubtful. 'It's an awfully big bed, Brodie. If you had a pillow-bolster we could share it,' she offered, unable to resist a down payment on revenge for his making her blush.

Emmy realised, but far too late, that she should have resisted, taking a step back as Brodie's eyes flared with anger, and with something else, something far more dangerous. She had done something very foolish. That was nothing new; she was famous for it. But this time she didn't quite know how to handle the outcome of her foolishness as Brodie slowly advanced on her.

'Share it?'

She took another step back, and another, before she finally came to a halt. Retreating was not in her nature. But it was a real effort to stand her ground when Brodie was up close with a six-inch height advantage and an edge to his voice that would have cut glass. But stand her ground she did, and launched a counter-offensive. 'Like they did in the Middle Ages?' she offered. 'A sword dividing the bed?'

'A sword? Wasn't that terribly dangerous?'

'You're missing the point, Brodie. It was symbolic. A true knight errant wouldn't cross the dividing line, even if the sword was sheathed. For safety,' she added, in case he should think she meant something else.

'I've already told you, Emmy. I'm no knight errant.' He took another step towards her. 'But it's an interesting idea. Perhaps a couple of pillows would do the trick.'

'No, Brodie,' she said quickly, putting out her hand to stop him coming any nearer. 'I was joking . . . '

Her palm collided with the tight

muscle of his chest but it did nothing to impede his progress, and as the warmth of his body seeped into her through her hand, along her arm, until her entire body seemed to be heating up from within, her fingers closed over his T-shirt, bunching it in her fist, holding it tight.

'Joking?' he enquired softly.

For a moment she thought she had a chance, and opened her mouth to reinforce her contention. But he stroked the backs of his long, slender fingers slowly and gently from her throat to her chin, mesmerising her with his touch, and a delicious languor stole through her body as he captured her chin. Then he began to trace a slow, sensuous line across her bottom lip with the tip of his thumb. It was like that moment in the car when he had so nearly kissed her. When she had, for one crazy moment, wanted him to kiss her more than anything else in the world. She still did, and when she saw the reflection of her own heart in his eyes Emerald Carlisle trembled.

'What is there to joke about, Emmy?' he finally asked her, his voice no longer diamond bright, but soft, like cobwebs tearing.

Brodie knew she had been teasing him with her invitation and he had planned to tease her right back, nothing more. If he had given the matter any thought he might have expected a slap for his impertinence, outraged virtue from a woman who had declared her determination to marry the man she loved, no matter what. But the tiny shiver as he touched her lip felt like an earthquake beneath his thumb. The shock waves of it ran up his arm and through his body and nothing mattered beyond the moment.

That was when Tom Brodie stopped thinking and did what he quite suddenly realised he had been wanting to do from the instant he had set eyes on Emerald Carlisle clinging to that damned drainpipe.

Emmy realised too late that it had been a mistake to stand her ground. She should have kept retreating. At least with her back to the wall she could have said she had done everything she could to avoid the results of her own stupidity. Custer had made a stand, and look what had happened to him. Oh, yes, indeed, there was no doubt about it, stopping had been a serious mistake, and now there was nowhere to run, and even if there had been she was transfixed, held prisoner in the magnetic force field Brodie seemed to be generating while he slowly lowered his head until his lips were level with hers.

And as he held her gaze with his hot grey eyes, her entire body captive to the crook of one finger beneath her chin, she slammed her eyes shut and expelled an involuntary groan through lips that she knew were too soft, too inviting. By the time she had decided she ought to do something about that, it was too late.

The kiss began with a touch as light

as his thumb trace, the petal-soft brush of his mouth as his lips discovered hers in a slow, seductive tango that stole away any lingering thoughts of resistance. Her lips parted as his tongue dipped against her teeth, and instinctively her free arm wound about his neck.

For a moment Brodie revelled in the sweetness of her mouth, her softness, the scent of her skin and her hair brushing against his cheek as she clung to him. The hand at her chin slipped behind her head, his fingers sliding through her hair to cup her nape. His other hand was at her waist, drawing her closer into his body as it tightened with desire. He wanted Emerald Carlisle, and in that lost moment, when the air stood still about them, he knew that she was his for the taking.

Then his masculine back-up system, the one that knew all the pitfalls, all the traps for the unwary male, kicked in, cruelly reminding him that he was older and supposedly a whole lot wiser than this girl in his arms, this girl whose interests it was his duty to protect.

When Gerald Carlisle had instructed him to do anything required to stop his daughter from marrying Kit Fairfax, taking her to his bed, Brodie felt certain, was not what the man had had in mind.

As he stiffened and pulled back Emmy gave a faint mewl of protest, and for a moment he considered consigning Gerald Carlisle to the devil, along with his conscience and quite possibly his career. Only the certain knowledge that she had been teasing him, had never intended things to go this far, stopped him. So why did he feel as he let her go that she had won? That it was giddy girl, one, wiser and older lawyer, nil?

Because this was a game he could never win?

Perhaps it was time he remembered that lawyers weren't supposed to play games. And that Emerald Carlisle would dare anything to get her own way.

He raised his head and looked down his long, straight nose at her. 'That's quite a sense of humour you've got, Emmy. And you've a nice line in distraction, but since your passport is locked away in my safe your sacrifice would be pointless. That is if you're still planning to go ahead with the wedding?'

He had finally persuaded his reluctant fingers to release her and he took a step back, just to be on the safe side. 'You *had* remembered that you're desperate to marry Kit Fairfax?' he said, to punish himself as much as her. Then, more harshly, as he suddenly realised what she had been doing, just how far she would go to get her own way, 'Or is the wedding just this month's attempt at winding up your father? I'd rather you told me now, because I've got better things to do than — '

'Desperate,' Emerald flung at him, with just the slightest crack in her voice. His expression suggested doubt, and who could blame him for that? she asked herself. Damn Hollingworth for going to Scotland. She wouldn't have had all this trouble with Hollingworth. She certainly wouldn't have made the terrible mistake of kissing him. But then, he wouldn't have let her escape down the drainpipe in the first place. 'I'm going to marry Kit as soon as possible,' she declared, sounding rather more than desperate in her need to convince Brodie of her sincerity. 'And there's nothing you can do to stop me.'

'No?' He reached out and pressed the tips of his fingers against her lips. Cool fingers that smelt of good soap and in some indefinable way of *him*. 'I'm certainly going to try,' he said. 'Whatever it takes.' Then he crossed to the night table and bent to unplug the telephone. As he straightened he caught the smallest smile of satisfaction cross her lips. She assumed he was removing the telephone to prevent her from making calls, assumed that she had got away with her call from the kitchen phone. Well, that was good.

But, while it was true that he didn't want her making any more unauthorised telephone calls, his intention in removing the bedroom phone was actually to prevent her from listening to his own call. He wrapped the wire slowly around the receiver and then crossed to the bedroom door.

'Goodnight, Emmy. Sleep well,' he said, before he pulled the door shut behind him with a decisive click.

Emmy closed her eyes, gritted her teeth and clenched her hands into tight little fists as a deep, shuddering breath racked her. Then very deliberately she forced herself to relax, and let go of the desperate urge to erupt in temper; after all she had nobody but herself to blame for what had happened.

Under the circumstances, flirting with Brodie had been quite unforgivable. And totally stupid. If he even suspected what she was up to the game would be over before it had begun.

But flirting with Brodie had an edge

to it, an excitement that was dangerously addictive. For a moment there she'd had only one thought in her mind, and she suspected Brodie had been light-years ahead of her. She glanced at his enormous bed as she undressed, pulled on an old rugby jersey that she wore as a nightshirt.

Light-years. But she had been catching up with him fast.

Then, smiling a touch ruefully as she threw back the quilt, she decided that they could have managed without a pillow-bolster to make a barrier between them and still have been perfectly chaste. It was, after all, an awfully big bed. But then Brodie was an awfully good-looking man, so presumably he wouldn't ever need to be lonely in it.

But that was a horribly disturbing thought, and as she slipped beneath the freshly laundered cover, Emmy discovered that she absolutely hated the idea.

★ ★ ★

Brodie returned to the kitchen and, crossing to the wall-mounted telephone, lifted the receiver and pressed 'redial'. After a moment or two the call was answered.

'Directory enquiries, which town?'

He stared at the receiver. *Directory enquiries?* 'I'm sorry, I misdialled,' he said, and hung up. Of all the devious women ... She'd obviously dialled Directory Enquiries after her call so that he wouldn't be able to check who she had rung. No wonder she had looked so damned pleased with herself.

More fool him for thinking that anything involving Miss Emerald Carlisle could be that easy. It seemed that if he wanted to find Kit Fairfax he had no choice but to go with her to France.

He rang his secretary. 'Jenny? I'm sorry to call so late, but I'm going to be out of the office for the rest of the week, running an errand for Gerald Carlisle. I'll leave you to rearrange my appointments, but there are some things I need you to do as a matter of urgency. First, there's a car I borrowed . . . '

*　*　*

'Emmy?' She opened her eyes at the tap on the door, the sound of her name. Then she closed them again, quickly. Sun was streaming in through the high-arched windows and it was far too bright after what had been a decidedly restless night. She rolled onto her stomach and buried her face in the pillow. The tap on the door was repeated, louder this time, imperative in its demand.

'Go away, Brodie,' she mumbled. But the pillow apparently muffled her words because behind her the door opened. 'I said, go away. I haven't finished sleeping.'

'I've brought you a cup of tea. You can wake up while I'm in the shower.'

'I don't want to wake up.'

'You don't have any choice. I've managed to get a couple of seats on the eight-twenty-seven train from Waterloo.'

Eight-twenty-seven? For a moment she lay perfectly still and ignored him. With trains leaving for all points south during the entire day, he had to choose the early-morning one? How efficient. How really, wonderfully, bloody efficient.

'Great,' she mumbled.

'It was that or the six-fifty-three. I didn't think you'd appreciate being woken at five.'

He was right about that. Even so. 'I thought they went every hour,' she grumbled into the pillow.

'They do to Paris, but we're changing at Lille. I've booked through to Marseilles, and we can hire a car when we arrive.'

'Marseilles? Why Marseilles?'

'You said the South of France,' he pointed out gently. 'If you'd like to be more specific . . . ?' he invited.

'I suppose Marseilles will do as well as anywhere.' Brodie was obviously still one step ahead of her, but not that far ahead.

'I just knew you'd be pleased.'

And because Emmy realised that under the circumstances she *should* be pleased — and because she knew he wasn't about to let her go back to sleep — she finally turned over, sat up and pushed the hair back from her face.

She was rather glad she'd made the effort. If you had to have an early-morning wake-up call, Brodie — hair tousled from sleep, his jaw so dark with the overnight growth of his beard that she wanted to reach out and rub her palm over it — was a whole lot more appealing than an alarm clock. She eased herself up the pillow and reached for the mug he was holding out to her, turning on a smile of lambent brightness. Marseilles was a big city. Anything might happen in Marseilles.

She glanced at the gold Cartier Panther on her wrist. It was just a little after six-thirty. Instead of groaning, she sipped her tea and said, 'Hadn't you better get a move on if we're going to catch that train? You've got fifteen minutes, Brodie, then the bathroom's mine.'

'If we shared it would save time.'

The casual way he said it jolted Emmy. She had known all along it would be crazy to underestimate the man. He had said he would stop the wedding whatever it took. If he'd decided that seduction was the easiest way, she was in big trouble.

She lowered her lashes, demure as a nun. 'I make it a rule never to share a bathroom with a man I've only just met,' she said.

'Just a bed?'

By the time she had absorbed the insult, opened her mouth to protest her innocence, Brodie had removed himself to the bathroom and shut the door fast behind him. She thought she might throw her mug, tea and all, at it, but since he would undoubtedly insist on her clearing up the mess she changed her mind and drank it instead. But she wouldn't forget.

She swung her legs over the edge of

the bed and opened her bag, considering what she would wear for the long train journey south, with the weather getting hotter every mile of the way. After a moment she shook out a short dark green bias-cut dress with tiny sleeves and a sprinkling of tiny ivory spots. It was fresh, neat and cool, and today she'd need to be all of those.

She gathered her underwear, sandals and matching handbag, into which she transferred everything she would need from the shoulder bag she had been using the night before. It was a pity about her passport, she thought as she flipped through her wallet, checking the francs she had collected from the bank a couple of days earlier.

Emmy glanced at the bathroom door. The shower had stopped a while ago and there was no time to dither. She took five one-hundred franc notes from her wallet and wrapped them up in the froth of ivory silk underwear that she had piled on the bed beside her dress.

She would have to get up very early

in the morning to outsmart Brodie, she decided. Fortunately, he had been a most efficient alarm clock.

★ ★ ★

The train was comfortable and Brodie had booked first-class seats. Well, why wouldn't he when her father would pick up the bill? Even so, Emmy was beginning to regret faking her fear of flying. It hadn't got her what she'd wanted and now she would have to sit next to Brodie for the best part of seven hours. Under normal circumstances that would not have been a hardship; normally she would have regarded the opportunity to flirt at length with a man like Brodie as the most delightful prospect.

These, however, were not normal circumstances, which was why, on arrival at Waterloo International, she had headed straight for the book stall and picked up three paperbacks. She wasn't about to risk taking just one book that she might hate after three pages. She'd turned to Brodie. 'I'll need some money to pay for these,' she had said, abruptly.

It was the first time she had deigned to speak to him since he had confiscated her credit cards and all her money except small change. She had anticipated the move, but sustained indignation had been the only possible response. If she had been too meek he would have smelt a rat, and, since he had already had a demonstration of her most likely hiding place, it wouldn't have taken him long to find the five hundred francs hidden in her bra. She wished she had dared to take more, but that would have left too little money in her wallet.

It was a small victory, but she was pleased with it. And she was determined to take the first opportunity to put it to good use.

'I was beginning to think we were going to spend our entire journey in silence,' he'd said, taking the books from her and paying for them.

'We are,' she'd replied. 'You'd better get something for yourself.'

Brodie had shrugged. 'I've got plenty of work to keep me occupied. All done here?' he'd asked, handing her the books, but keeping the receipt. 'No mints, chocolates, barley sugar?' She'd glared at him. 'Then we might as well board the train.'

Breakfast was served, and was passed in deliberate silence on Emmy's part, in apparent oblivion on Brodie's. He ate absent-mindedly, more interested in the document he was reading than her apparent bout of the sulks.

'It's incredibly rude to read at the table,' Emmy declared, finally driven to protest at this lack of attention.

He turned, surprised. 'Oh, I'm sorry. I didn't think you wanted to talk. At least, not to me.' He closed the file he had been reading and waited.

She felt foolish. Having protested that she was being ignored, she now had to say something, but under that cool, slightly distant gaze all she could think of was last night, when his eyes had been anything but cool and he had kissed her. Desperate, she made a gesture towards the papers he had been reading and sent her orange juice flying. She watched in horror as the thick, pithy liquid spread over the file and began to seep towards the legal documents it contained.

The steward, spotting this minor catastrophe, immediately mopped up the worst of the spill and whisked away the cloth. Brodie took the papers from the folder, wiped them on his napkin and handed the folder to the steward. 'Perhaps you could dispose of this?'

'Of course, sir. And I'll bring the young lady another glass of orange juice.'

'No,' Emmy said, quickly. 'There's no need. Thank you.' The man departed and she turned to Brodie. 'I'm sorry. Are your papers ruined?'

'No. They're fine.' He reached for his document case and slipped them inside, but not before she'd seen the name on the top sheet.

'Good grief, is he your client?' she asked. He flickered a glance at her and she realised he was just a touch amused that she was impressed. 'Since when have multi-millionaire pop stars been clients of a stuffy old firm like Broadbent, Hollingworth & Maunsell?' she demanded.

'Since I've been a partner.'

'Oh, I see.'

'I doubt it.'

It wasn't in Emmy's nature to sustain a feud, or remain silent for long no matter what the provocation, and this was her opportunity to break the ice. 'Then tell me.'

Brodie regarded her for a moment, the wide, innocent gold-flecked eyes set beneath dark, delicately winged brows. Despite her red hair, Emmy's lashes and brows were dark and lustrous against a creamy complexion. She was very beautiful. And all the more dangerous because of it. Despite that, or maybe because he enjoyed dicing with danger, he accepted this tentative olive branch.

'I've known Chas since primary school,' he said.

'Chas?'

'That's his name. Charles Potter.'

'I can understand why he changed it.'

'When he was offered his first contract, he couldn't afford a proper solicitor so his mother suggested he ask my advice — since I was going to study law.'

'You're kidding?'

'We don't all have the benefit of being born with a whole canteen of silver spoons in our mouths, Emmy.'

'Oh.' For a moment she looked crestfallen. Then, 'Tell me about the contract.'

'It looked impressive — the numbers were big, and it was the sort of contract no eighteen-year-old musician would have turned down. A lot of them didn't and have lived to regret it.'

'You advised him not to sign?'

'The contract was for the number of albums recorded. It didn't have a time scale. It seemed to me that if he was still recording in twenty years' time it might just be on the same contract. I suggested he went back to the company and asked for a contract for five albums. They wanted him, and, let's be honest, how many pop stars last that long? They agreed. He was impressed. And I was relieved,' he admitted. 'As a result I'm still checking out his contracts, only these days I rely on more than a hunch to make sure they're watertight.'

'Which is just as well since he's a multi-million-pound corporation with his own recording company. It's a nice story, Brodie. Do you still hand out advice for free?'

'I get my best clients that way and some of my worst ones.' She raised one of those glossy brows. 'I run a legal clinic at an advice centre in one of the less salubrious parts of London.'

'A regular Mr Nice Guy.'

'One who'll give you some advice for free right now.' His face was grave, his eyes serious. 'Catch the next train home, Emmy. Rushing into marriage is always a mistake, and if Fairfax is genuine he'll wait for your father to come round.'

Emmy reached for a book, but before she opened it she gave him an enigmatic little smile. 'You think it's going to be easy to talk Kit into taking my father's money, don't you?'

'Do I?'

For a moment she held his gaze. 'You're wrong about him, you know.'

Brodie was startled by the glowing sincerity with which she spoke, but she was right. He had been assuming, like Carlisle, that it would simply be a matter of numbers ... how many pound notes it would take to buy the man off. As Emmy settled back to read, however, he put himself in Kit Fairfax's shoes. If Emmy loved *him* just how much would it take to make him change his mind?

It was then that he realised he'd better give some serious thought about his next move if the man refused to take the bribe.

*　*　*

It was early evening by the time the train pulled into Marseilles. Another half an hour before they were sitting in the comfortable Renault that Brodie had hired.

He turned to her. 'Well, Emmy, we're in the South of France. Where now?'

'Head north,' she said. 'Then east.'

'North and then east?' He regarded her with a degree of amusement. 'You'll forgive me, but that isn't very precise. Where exactly are we going?'

'I'll give you directions as we go,' she hedged.

'Not directions like that, you won't. It'll be dark in a couple of hours and I have no intention of ending up lost on some remote track miles from anywhere.' Which was what she undoubtedly had in mind.

'Just head north, Brodie. I'll tell you when to turn off. I'm really good with directions.'

He hadn't expected her to tell him where they were going; in fact he had rather been banking on her obstinacy. 'In the dark?' he pressed. 'Honest?'

'Of course,' she said, not quite meeting his eyes. He gave her a thoughtful look before he started the engine and, pulling out of the garage, headed for the nearest intersection. It was then that Emmy abandoned her careless pose. 'You've taken the wrong turning, Brodie!' she declared as he headed towards the old port area of the city. 'I said *north*.'

5

Brodie was unmoved. ''North' is not good enough, Emmy. I've been sitting in a train since first thing this morning and I'm not about to be driven all over France on some wild-goose chase of yours. We'll spend the night in Marseilles and set off first thing in the morning. Once you've told me exactly where we're headed.'

She stared at him, clearly not believing her own ears. 'I thought you were desperate to get this finished with.'

'I am.' Then he shrugged. 'But not so desperate that I'm prepared to drive off into the night without any idea of where I'm going. Besides, it does seem a shame to come so close to the home of bouillabaisse and not treat ourselves to a dish.'

He'd been in an odd mood ever since they'd left this morning, Emmy thought. As if he knew something that she didn't, and it bothered her. But she knew why he was doing this. She had refused to tell him exactly where they were going, afraid that he would find some way to leave her behind and take off into the interior to deal with Kit without any interference from her. After all he thought she was penniless and entirely in his hands.

Well, she would let him think it. It would probably be a lot easier getting away from him in a busy city like Marseilles than out in the country. But it wouldn't do to let him see she didn't mind that much.

'I hate bouillabaisse,' she said, sitting back in her seat, folding her arms and staring out of the opposite window.

'It's not obligatory. I know a restaurant down by the old port where I'm sure you'll find something to your taste. The view, if nothing else. Perhaps we should take a boat ride out to the Château D'If in the morning? I'll show you the cell in which the Count of

Monte Cristo was incarcerated if you like.'

'Don't be ridiculous, Brodie, *The Count of Monte Cristo* is a novel. Fiction. Dante wasn't *real*.'

'I know,' he replied, teasing her gently. 'Neither was Sherlock Holmes, but people still write to him at his Baker Street lodgings.'

'Anyone would think *you* were on holiday,' she declared, crossly. 'My future is at stake here. Aren't you taking it seriously?'

'I am finding it rather difficult,' he confessed. 'Hollingworth might be able to justify a jaunt like this as business but then he's more used to this sort of thing than I am.' He paused, waited; she didn't reply. 'You have done this before?' he prompted.

She blushed. 'I'm sure my father gave you all the details.'

'Some,' he agreed. Gerald Carlisle had told him that Emmy had fallen for a smooth-talking fortune-hunter who had eloped with her from a villa where they had been staying with friends. Brodie suspected that it had been more a case of a summer romance that had got out of control; a real fortune-hunter would have taken a great deal more money to dislodge.

'I was barely eighteen, Brodie,' she said defensively as the silence continued. 'A child.' She set her lips in a firm line. 'This time I know exactly what I'm doing.'

'Maybe you do, Emmy.' And when *he'd* worked out what exactly she was doing it would be soon enough to confront Fairfax. 'But, since I had planned to take a few days off this month, I've decided to combine business with pleasure.'

'Oh, really? And do you always bring work with you when you're on holiday?'

'I brought you.'

She glared at him. 'What did you do, Brodie? Ring your secretary in the middle of the night and get her to rearrange your schedule? Just like that?' She snapped her fingers.

'I wasn't given much choice. Apart from a diary full of appointments that needed to be changed, I had to organise the return of the car I borrowed after you — ' Emmy glared at him, daring him to say the word 'stole'. 'After you helped yourself to mine.' He grinned. 'I think you owe Jenny a bunch of flowers at the very least for getting her out of bed. Make it a big one and I won't say another word about it.'

She wasn't proud of taking his car and didn't like being continually reminded of it. 'Is that a promise?'

'Cross my heart.' He took one hand off the wheel and sketched a cross above his heart.

'Then it's a deal.' Emmy remained silent while Brodie wove through the evening traffic and pulled into the space in front of a small hotel. 'You're serious, aren't you?' she said as he flipped the release on his seatbelt. 'Why don't you just forget about me and take your holiday?'

'Because I'm very conscientious.

However, I'm quite prepared to relax tonight and forget why we're here. Why don't you try and do the same?' Emmy regarded Brodie with suspicion. She didn't think he was on holiday; she thought that he was being horribly devious about something. But Brodie smiled and offered her his hand. 'Come on. You might as well accept that the only travelling we're doing tonight is going to be a gentle promenade below the fort to admire the sunset over Vieux Port. I promise you, it won't hurt a bit. You might even enjoy it.'

Emmy thought that he was probably right, but as she took his hand and allowed him to help her from the car she reminded herself not to let it show too much.

★ ★ ★

Brodie, Emmy realised as they entered the small but charming hotel, had never intended to drive into the interior that night. The proprietor, Monsieur Girard, was clearly an old friend, greeting him with warmth and enthusiasm but certainly no surprise.

She strained to follow Brodie's excellent French as he signed the registration card, but the two men were speaking too quickly for her own inept schoolgirl version of the language.

'Your secretary is remarkably efficient,' Emmy said, just a little sourly, as it became obvious that his decision to stay overnight in Marseilles had nothing to do with her reluctance to tell him exactly where they were headed.

Brodie caught her look, gave the slightest of shrugs. 'I knew we wouldn't arrive until late afternoon so I asked her to ring ahead and reserve a room for me.' He pushed the card he had filled in across the reception desk. 'You should learn to overcome your fear of flying, Emmy. We could have been here several hours ago and you would by now have been in the arms of your own true love.' He said that with a certain cynicism. Presumably her enthusiastic reponse when he kissed her had reinforced his view that she was simply winding up her father. That had been a mistake, she acknowledged, but an understandable one, surely? The assured manner of that kiss had suggested that he was used to enthusiasm. 'Have you tried hypnosis?' he asked.

'Hypnosis?'

'I believe it can be quite effective in dealing with irrational fears. If, of course, your fear is genuine.' He clearly wasn't convinced about that either. He took the key the proprietor handed him and, picking up both their bags in one hand, headed for the antiquated lift with its wrought-iron gates.

'One key?' she demanded.

Brodie's jaw tightened. 'One key. And you'd better hope there's a bolster, Emmy. This is an old-fashioned hotel; they don't go in for twin beds.'

'Really?' She stepped into the lift. 'Then I hope, for your sake, Brodie, that the floor is comfortable.'

'It wouldn't be the first time I'd slept

135

on a floor. I just hope there isn't a draught under the door.'

Emmy smiled so much that it felt as if her face was cracking in half. 'You think I'd make a bolt for it? In Marseilles, in the middle of the night?'

'It sounds unlikely when you put it like that. However, your track record to date suggests I would be foolish to ignore the possibility. And just in case there's a handy drainpipe I'm warning you now that I'll have all our documents and money locked in the hotel safe overnight.' And, apparently able to read her mind, he continued, 'You may not need your passport to travel now, Emmy. You'll certainly need it to get married.' He paused. 'Along with your birth certificate, an affidavit of residence in France, a prenuptial medical certificate, a solicitor's certificate regarding a marriage contract, a Certificate of Law from the British Embassy in Paris — that is if you haven't already applied for one from the Foreign and Commonwealth Office

— the declaration of forenames — '

'You've been doing your homework,' she said, interrupting what was obviously going to be a lengthy list.

'It's my legal training. You only have one chance to get it right. And the French do take marriage very seriously — as you'd have discovered if you'd done your homework before starting out on this madcap scheme. It would have saved us both a lot of trouble,' he told her as the lift finally jolted to a stop.

'Trouble is my middle name,' she retorted. 'Didn't my father tell you that?'

'We didn't discuss names, but according to the file he gave me you were registered at birth simply as Emerald Louise Victoria. Was Trouble a baptismal addition?' He opened the gate for her and, apparently not expecting an answer to his question, said, 'After you, Miss Carlisle.'

He was confident that he had her, she thought as she stepped from the lift.

Well, that was good. He would relax. He would be less cautious. And for now she would be very, very good.

But there was no need for pretence as she looked around the delightful suite of rooms they had been allocated on the first floor, overlooking Vieux Port. Old-fashioned provincial French, with heavy ornate furniture, the sitting room and bedroom were charming.

And, since the sitting room was furnished with a large and comfortable-looking sofa, he had obviously been just teasing about sharing the huge, inviting bed that dominated the inner room.

'Didn't your secretary query just one suite of rooms, Brodie?' she asked, glancing into the bathroom.

'My secretary isn't supposed to know that you are with me,' he pointed out. Which didn't quite answer her question, she noticed. But then, he *was* a lawyer.

'Then who did she think the other seat on the train was for?'

'In the interests of discretion, I

decided to book the seats on the train myself.'

'You're hoping to keep the whole thing quiet?' she enquired as she turned back to him.

'If you want to make a spectacle of yourself in the tabloids, Emmy, I really couldn't care less. I am simply acting as your father's agent — '

'You mean you're just obeying orders?' Brodie's slate eyes hardened to granite, his face darkening ominously. And he was right to be angry. She knew that it had been an unforgivable, hateful thing to say. Emmy, immediately repentant, took half a step towards him. 'Brodie . . . ' she began, but he cut off her apology.

'In a situation that is totally repellent to me. However, since I wholeheartedly agree with his sentiments when it comes to avaricious men who take advantage of young women cursed with an abundance of wealth, I will do everything I possibly can to carry out his wishes. Not for him, but for you.'

And, picking up his briefcase, he crossed to the door. 'I'll leave you to use the bathroom first, Emmy. I suggest you take the opportunity to wash your mouth out while you're in there.'

She couldn't let him go like that, and she rushed across the room, grasping the sleeve of his jacket to detain him. 'I'm sorry, Brodie,' she blurted out. 'Truly.'

'So am I.' He glanced down pointedly at her fingers and she instantly removed them. 'Take your time in the bathroom. I'm going to have a drink.'

Emmy flinched as the door closed with a firmness that would have equalled a slam from anyone less controlled, and she leaned back against it with a little shudder. 'Damn,' she said. 'Damn.' Her father had no doubt told him that she was a spoilt brat and now, with one stupid remark, she had apparently confirmed it.

She realised that she couldn't bear to have Brodie believe that. She didn't want him to think she was a thoughtless girl who was simply going out of her way to give her father the maximum amount of grief. But short of telling him the truth what on earth could she do?

Nothing. She'd already learned that people believed what they wanted to believe, and most people chose to believe that she was just like her mother — wild, irresponsible and selfish. But she wasn't. Oh, she'd had her moments, but nothing worse than most girls of her age. But her wealth, and a mother with a string of lovers, had put her under the spotlight so that every minor indiscretion was magnified out of all proportion.

What was so unfair, so bloody unfair, was that her mother would never have got herself into this kind of situation. Or, if she had, would have quit at the first sign of difficulty.

But Brodie would discover that Emerald Carlisle was not a quitter; unlike her mother she would never run out on a friend, or her family, or a lover just because the going got tough. She'd see this through to the end, and she refused to allow either her father or Brodie to stop her. Only Kit could do that, which was why she simply had to get to him before Brodie. It would be hard enough even then . . .

Why was it that life threw you these horrible little trials to test your determination? Just when you were sailing happily along without a care in the world, when plans had been made, when putting them into practice had seemed to be a piece of cake?

Why on earth had Kit decided he simply had to go to France at that very moment, for instance? Nothing she could say or do had been able to dissuade him. He'd just dropped one of those absent-minded kisses on her forehead, told her not to worry about him, that everything would sort itself out. But she knew that Kit's optimism was misplaced. Everything would not sort itself out, it never did unless someone did something to give it a helping hand.

Still, that had been a minor inconvenience; it had only become a disaster when her father had demonstrated an unsuspected ability to think on his feet. Or maybe not. Once she had decided what she would do, she had flaunted Kit quite shamelessly . . . even staying overnight at his studio once she had realised he was being checked out by her father's pet investigator. And because of that her father had been ready for her. She wondered idly what he would have done if, as Brodie had suggested, she'd revealed a three-day licence for a register office wedding . . . Have Mark Reed snatch her off the pavement and bundle her down to Honeybourne in the boot of his Bentley?

Then, as if she hadn't enough to cope with, Hollingworth, a man with a severe imagination bypass, a man she could rely on to do exactly what her father said without question, had departed for Scotland and the grouse moors, leaving her to the tender mercy of Tom Brodie, whose imagination was in full working

order and who didn't respond predict-
ably when someone pulled his strings.
In fact she was willing to wager that he
hadn't responded to string-pulling since
the midwife had cut the umbilical cord.

She brushed a stupid tear from her
cheek and stood up. Tomorrow she
would have to escape her clever
watchdog in order to get to Kit before
him. Tonight she and Brodie were in
Marseilles, with an evening stroll on the
agenda followed by a candlelit supper
and a chance to redeem herself just a
little in his eyes. And finally a smile
softened the determined line of her
mouth. Tonight she would be good.

But not for another few minutes.
She'd use the time Brodie had given
her to check the layout of the hotel. It
would undoubtedly be the only chance
she'd get.

★　★　★

Brodie had discarded his jacket and was
stretched out on a pavement chair

soaking up the lingering heat of the sun. He stared at the glass of *pastis* he was holding, its cloudy depths as obscure as the problems raised by Emerald Carlisle. He shifted uncomfortably. What on earth was he doing, chasing around the South of France with a runaway heiress, for heaven's sake? The whole thing was like some 1940s romantic comedy with Cary Grant. Except there was nothing funny about the situation, at least not from his point of view.

He specialised in Corporate Law. It was serious stuff. He took his work seriously. This nonsense . . . and Emerald Carlisle . . . who could possibly take her seriously? But he already knew.

He closed his eyes. What on earth was the matter with him? He wasn't in the habit of losing his head over a pretty face. Yet that he had was demonstrable by the fact that they were here together in Marseilles, sharing a hotel suite, when common sense suggested that he should have phoned her father the moment he'd caught up with her in her flat. Or before that — called him from the café where they had stopped. Or simply turned around and taken her back to Honeybourne the moment he'd realised she had stowed away in his car. So why hadn't he? Why had he connived with her escape in the first place?

Above the mingled smells of the traffic and the harbour her scent lingered in his memory, the way she had felt in his arms, the taste of her mouth as she had melted against him, and he knew why.

His hand tightened around the glass. She hadn't meant it, he reminded himself. She had been desperate to distract him, bewitch him . . . and for a moment she had succeeded. The way she had looked up at him just now with those huge green-gold eyes as she had tried to apologise; it had taken every ounce of will-power not to take her into his arms, to just walk away.

Damn it, he should have driven her

straight to Fairfax and sorted the whole thing out tonight. He'd brought her here to delay her, not for her own good, but for his. Because he wanted to get to know her. Understand what was driving her. There *was* something. And he could swear it wasn't undying love for Kit Fairfax. Or maybe he just wanted to believe that . . .

The glass disintegrated in his hands, showering him with *pastis* and shards of glass.

He was immediately descended upon by Madame Girard, who rushed out to cluck and coo over him, checking his hand for cuts while the waiter swept the glass from the pavement. But there was no damage except for a damp patch on his trousers, and he refused a replacement for his drink; there were no answers to his problems to be found at the bottom of a glass.

He would be much better occupied calling his office to see what messages Mark Reed had left for him, if any.

But Mark Reed had no news for him.

Gerald Carlisle, however, had left several messages. 'He's desperate to know if you've managed to speak to a man called Fairfax,' Jenny told him. 'I take it you know what he's talking about?'

'Yes, unfortunately. And the answer is no. I've discovered he's in the South of France and I hope to find him tomorrow. That's all. Anything else?'

'Mmm. He asked if you'd said anything about seeing his daughter, given her a lift into London last night, perhaps? I said you hadn't mentioned anything to me.' She paused. 'It *was* just one suite of rooms you asked me to book for you?'

'There is nothing wrong with your hearing, Jenny.'

'No. I thought not. Only I wondered. What with all that business about your car. You never did explain why you'd had to borrow that little purple VW.'

'No, Jenny, I didn't. And if you continue to interrogate me like some overpaid QC I'll never tell you what happened. I promise you, you'll be sorry.'

'No, I won't. I'll ring Betty and ask her.'

'Betty?'

'What a sweet lady. She rang to thank you for the prompt return of her car and for all the lovely presents.' Jenny paused. 'She also gave me a message to pass on. She asked me to tell you . . . no, hold on, I wrote it down because I didn't want to get this wrong . . . she said 'The cards are warning against taking affairs of the heart at face value'. She said to tell you that 'Nothing is what it seems'. Does that make sense to you?'

'As much sense as anything else that's happened this week,' he replied caustically. 'If she calls again ask her if the cards can locate Kit Fairfax.'

'I won't wait for her to ring, Tom. I'm going to call her right now. Do you want me to tell Mr Carlisle that his daughter is with you? Or would you rather he didn't know?'

'I can get another secretary any time, Jenny,' he warned. 'I'll ask the agency to replace you with one of those leggy blondes — '

'And here was me thinking leggy redheads were the flavour of the month. I'll give your love to Betty, shall I?'

* * *

Returning to their suite, Brodie discovered that Emerald had taken him at his word when he'd told her not to hurry in the bathroom. She was wrapped in a bathrobe, her curly hair still damp from the shower, when he tapped at the bedroom door and was answered with a cheery, 'Come in.'

He stopped abruptly in the doorway. 'I'm sorry, I thought you would have been dressed by now.'

'Did you?' She paused in the careful application of mascara to look up at him, and immediately noticed the damp patch above his knee. 'Did you enjoy your drink?'

'Not particularly.' He headed for the bathroom. 'If I pass my trousers out to you, will you give them to Madame Girard? She's waiting outside, desperate to give them a sponge and press.'

She put down her mascara wand and followed him to the bathroom door, leaning with her back to the architrave while she waited for him to remove them and pass them out to her. 'This is all delightfully intimate, Brodie,' she called back through the door. 'But do you think it was what my father had in mind when he instructed you to stop at nothing to prevent my marriage to Kit?'

'Stop at nothing?' Brodie didn't recall Gerald Carlisle couching his instructions in quite those terms. 'That seems rather desperate.'

'Desperate situations need desperate measures. Kit, you know, is not his idea of a suitable son-in-law.'

'I had already gathered that.' Brodie, wrapped in a bathrobe, began emptying his pockets onto a small table just inside the bathroom door. 'What exactly is wrong with the man?'

'Haven't you read that great big file he gave you?'

'Not all of it.'

'Just enough to know all my horrible names.'

'I haven't had a lot of time.' He certainly hadn't been able to bring himself to take it out and read it while she'd been sitting next to him on the train. In fact he didn't want to read it at all. He'd much rather hear Emerald's story from her own lips. Over dinner.

'Oh, well, let me enlighten you,' she said obligingly. 'Kit is an artist, which, on its own, is sufficient reason to rule him out of the son-in-law stakes, you understand. Then there's the problem of money. He doesn't have any — '

'Which is why he's about to lose his studio.'

'He's not going to lose his studio — '

'Not if he marries you.'

She glared at him. 'Finally, and probably worst of all . . . ' Brodie waited and she gave a wicked little shrug. 'Well, his hair comes down below his collar. Or would do, if he ever wore one.'

'Beyond the pale, without a doubt,' Brodie said dryly.

'You don't think that combination makes him a totally unsuitable husband?'

'Not necessarily — '

'Hollingworth would be very disappointed to hear you say that, Brodie, and so would my father. Are you sure you're the man for the job? It's not too late. You could still summon Hollingworth from his ritual Highland slaughter — '

'Just a totally unsuitable husband for you. While you, Miss Carlisle, would appear to be all Fairfax's dreams come true.' All *most men*'s dreams come true, if it came to that. *Without* the multi-million-pound inheritance from her grandmother.

'That's very cynical of you, Brodie. Don't you believe in true love?'

'Not when the advantages are so

loaded in one direction.'

'Only on paper. You haven't met Kit, yet,' she said, pushing herself away from the doorframe and turning to take the trousers from him. 'So you're in no position to judge. He's going to be a great artist one day.'

'With you as his muse? You don't strike me as the kind of woman to live a second-hand life in someone else's shadow.'

She threw him a startled glance. 'I'd better hand these over to *Madame* if we're going to eat tonight.'

'A good idea. And just in case it occurred to you to do something drastic to them, Emmy, I should advise you that I do have another pair.'

She laid one hand against her breast, looking thoroughly shocked. 'Nothing so dreadful had crossed my mind, Brodie.' Then she rather spoilt the effect by adding, 'But I'd seriously advise you not to put ideas into my head.'

He grinned. 'You don't need anyone

to put ideas into your head, Emmy. You've quite enough of your own.'

Emmy's answering smile was seraphic. 'A compliment, how sweet. But I promise I'll be good tonight. I'm hungry, and I have this strong suspicion that if I chop up your trousers with my nail scissors I won't be getting room service. I'll just be sent to bed without any supper.'

'You could be right. And I would consider it my duty to make sure you stayed there.' His own smile could scarcely be described as angelic. More like the devil in a good mood. 'You choose,' he said.

And suddenly she wasn't looking at him, challenging him. Instead her glance flickered self-consciously towards the big, cushion-heaped bed that dominated the room, and he saw a slow flush of colour steal into her cheeks before she once more turned her huge hazel eyes upon him. For the space of a heartbeat it seemed that the world stood still, a heartbeat in which nothing mattered but two people alone in a room . . . somewhere . . . Then a sharp rap on the sitting room door shattered the spell, and Emmy spun around and walked from the room without another word.

And Brodie turned and closed the bathroom door, leaning against it as he let out a long, slow breath. It was a long time since he'd felt an urgent need for a cold shower, but right now seemed like a good time. For a solicitor acting *in loco parentis*, he was spending altogether too much time in bedrooms with Emerald Carlisle.

Which, if she was as in love with Fairfax as she proclaimed, shouldn't have been a problem. So why was it? For both of them?

6

Emerald was shaking as she opened the door and handed Brodie's trousers to Madame Girard. She returned cautiously to the bedroom. But there was no sign of Brodie, just the sound of water running from beyond the bathroom door.

She wasted no more time, but slipped out of the bathrobe and stepped into the simplest pale peach silk jersey dress that skimmed over her figure, stopping well short of her knees. Far too short, and the neck scooped in a way that suddenly seemed recklessly flirtatious. And, dear God, how she wanted to flirt!

Oh, no. Not just flirt. Whenever Brodie was near her all she could think of was reaching out to touch him, feeling his skin beneath her fingers, against her body. And he felt the same way — she knew it, had seen it in his eyes just now. Whatever that flash of recognition between them as she had hung from the drainpipe had been, it was like an irresistible force drawing them together. And the more time they spent together, the stronger it became. There was only one place it could end, and her eyes were drawn once more to the bed.

Why now? Why now when it was all just so impossible?

She was shaking with the sheer force of her feelings; her hands were trembling. She couldn't possibly wait until tomorrow morning to make a dash for it. The way things were going, tomorrow might well be too late. It would have to be now. She cast around her for the car keys, then remembered that Brodie had emptied his pockets in the bathroom.

The shower was still running — inside the frosted-glass cubicle he wouldn't see her — but her heart was beating in her mouth as she slowly eased the door open a crack. His wallet, some loose change and the keys were lying on the small table just inside the door. She carefully lifted the keys and began to back out, then she stopped and helped herself to the wallet as well, taking a thousand francs. After all, she reasoned, he wouldn't be short of money — he had hers in safe keeping.

Then she grabbed her low-heeled sandals and tiny shoulder bag into which her precious five hundred francs had already been transferred. Yet still she hesitated, glancing at the bathroom door, hating to leave like this, knowing what he would think of her.

Then the water stopped and she caught her breath. Why on earth was she dithering? She had seconds, not hours, and Brodie would come after her, she had proof enough that he wouldn't hang about wringing his hands. He was a man of action. She hung onto that thought as she beat a hasty retreat down the stairs, ignoring a startled cry from Monsieur Girard as she passed him in the lobby.

Her fingers were shaking so much as she tried to fit the key to the lock of the car that she was afraid she would set off the alarm, but finally it slid home without incident and she flung herself into the driving seat, dropping her shoes and bag on the seat beside her.

'Deep breaths, Emmy,' she said. 'Deep breaths. He doesn't even know you've gone yet. And this time he won't know where you're going.' She glanced over the controls. They were all on the wrong side. Still, she'd been driving about her father's estate since she'd been able to reach the pedals with the help of a cushion. She would manage. She started the engine. It purred as gently as a contented kitten, and she carefully selected reverse. This was not the moment to demolish the front of the hotel.

She glanced behind her. Left or right? It was so confusing. Right . . . it was right . . . She looked . . . the road was miraculously clear, and she eased her foot down on the accelerator and began to move backwards.

'Emerald!' Brodie's voice thundered from the first-floor window in a manner that echoed a number of unpleasant incidences earlier in her life. The time she'd run away from school. The occasion on which she'd borrowed her father's Bentley to run down to the village shop for some hairspray. She'd been fifteen at the time. Or was it fourteen? The last time had been when she'd run away with Oliver Hayward . . .

She didn't hang around to discover if Brodie in a temper resembled her father in any other way. She jammed her foot down hard on the accelerator and swung out of the parking space. Behind her there was a screech of brakes and a crunch of rending metal that sent her flying forward. In her hurry she'd forgotten her seatbelt, but the airbag erupted with admirable efficiency, saving her from the worst effects of her own stupidity.

It did not, however, save her from a

torrent of Gallic abuse that she was fortunately largely unable to understand.

Besides, an angry Frenchman was nothing compared to what she could expect from Brodie. She looked up as, white with rage and shaking with fury, he wrenched the car door open.

'Are you hurt?' His voice was shaking too, she noticed. He had a smear of shaving cream beneath his right ear and he was standing in the street barefoot, wearing nothing but a bathrobe. And they were being rapidly surrounded by a crowd of onlookers, each of whom had an opinion about what had happened and was determined that someone should listen.

It was very loud and rather frightening, and all she wanted was for Brodie to hold her and tell her that it would be all right. But he wasn't about to do that. He was going to shout at her for being a stupid, irresponsible *girl*, and that was worse, because he was right. So she put her hands over her ears and closed her eyes.

But he took her hands away from her ears. 'Emmy?' Brodie's voice almost cracked, and she turned as she realised that he wasn't angry, that he couldn't care less about the car, or the crowd, or the fact that she had behaved like an absolute idiot and had no doubt brought down a whole barrel-load of trouble on their heads.

He was only concerned about her.

At that moment she could have thrown her arms about him and kissed him. Instead she just shook her head. 'No. I'm not hurt,' she said as a tiny shiver seemed to sweep over her from head to toe.

He noticed. 'You're sure?'

'I'm sure,' she snapped irritably. Much as she longed for him to hold her, kissing him was not an option.

But he must have put her irritation down to shock because, rather than responding in kind, he eased his arm gently beneath hers to help her out of the car, as if she were made of something very precious, very fragile. And she discovered that she needed the help as her legs buckled and she sagged against him. He put his other arm about her and held her against him.

'Emmy?' he repeated, more urgently.

Oh, God. He was so gentle, so concerned that she wanted to weep at the unfairness of it all, but as the tears squeezed from beneath her eyelids she laid her head against his chest so that he shouldn't see.

'I'm sorry, Brodie,' she muttered into the fluffy white towelling. 'I'm so sorry.'

He said something soothing, and she was almost sure he kissed the top of her head. That just made things ten times worse. Especially as the driver of the other car had come closer in order to abuse her more directly, and was perfectly happy to include Brodie in his insults.

But as she flinched Brodie began talking quietly to the man, and although she didn't understand every-thing he said she understood enough to

164

know that he was taking the blame, telling him that she had not been looking because she had been upset, because they had quarrelled.

The onlookers began murmuring amongst themselves, uttering wonderfully Gallic exclamations of understanding, warmly reminiscent of French wine commercials, and she caught phrases such as '*affaire de coeur*' spoken in a knowing manner. And then she was aware of a sudden and expectant hush.

'Emmy?' She glanced up. 'I'm afraid everyone is waiting for us to kiss and make up,' he murmured.

'Oh?'

He pushed the tumbled curls back from her cheek, gently brushing the tears from her lashes with the pad of his thumb. 'This is France, you see,' he said, as if that explained everything.

'I see. And if I kiss you it will help . . . ?'

In answer, he cradled her cheek in his hand. '*Je suis désolé, chérie* . . . ' he murmured softly, for the benefit of the onlookers. They clucked encouragingly but she didn't rush the moment.

'Don't be *désolé*, Brodie,' she said. 'I'm the one who should be apologising. I did promise to be good . . . '

'You did . . . but I assumed you had your fingers crossed.' His eyes were cloaked beneath heavy lids as he looked down at her.

'A girl has to take every opportunity that presents itself,' she said, by way of justification. 'You should have locked the bathroom door.'

'I thought I had. Apparently the lock doesn't work.'

'No, I'd already discovered that for myself.'

'Of course. Well, here comes the payoff and you'd better make this look convincing, sweetheart, because you weren't insured to drive that car, and if this fellow turns nasty no amount of your father's money will save you from a trip to the magistrates' court.'

'Not even with my own personal lawyer in tow?'

Her own personal lawyer did not look particularly happy about that. 'Your own personal lawyer can only offer advice. It's up to you whether you take it.'

'And he advises a passionate reconciliation?'

'Please, Emmy.' *Please, Emmy*. How blissful that sounded. 'Now,' he urged, 'they're getting impatient.'

But she needed no urging. Rocking up onto tiptoe, reaching up to put her arms around his neck, she looked straight into eyes as dark as rain-washed slate and then she closed her own and touched her lips to his. Around them the crowd drew in a single, audible breath. But Emmy didn't hear. All her senses were concentrated on Brodie. On the warmth of his skin beneath her fingers, the scent of his body, the taste of his mouth against hers.

His lips were cool and he made no move to deepen the kiss. He had just brushed his teeth and she could taste his toothpaste, clean, sharp and stimulating, against her lips, but she wanted more than this chaste salute, and so, she suspected, did the onlookers. Make it look convincing, he had said. Take your lawyer's advice . . . please. And for once it would be her pleasure to obey him.

Her lips parted softly, inviting his participation, and her tongue teased gently inside his lip. For a moment he remained quite still, as if transfixed by her touch. Then, without warning, Brodie took control, his mouth coming down hard on hers, meeting her invitation head-on until the desire she had been desperately trying to suppress since their eyes had met over her father's unsuspecting head pooled in her body and she melted against him.

It was madness, but it was blissful madness. But this had been Brodie's idea, and for a brief moment she could let herself go, forget any concern about betraying her feelings. This was one kiss she could enjoy without ever having to pretend and she was going to make the most of it.

After a few moments she became aware at some basic level of consciousness that the crowd were beginning to clap in time as the kiss was drawn out, then there was a long, juddering mass sigh as Brodie seemed to gather himself, easing back from the kiss.

Her eyes flickered open; she was suddenly afraid of what she might see in his eyes. Would he be angry with her? Disgusted, even, that she could declare love for one man and kiss another as if one of them were going to war? But he was simply staring down at her, his face a mask, betraying nothing.

Then he turned away to murmur something to Monsieur Girard, before bending to catch her behind the knees, lifting her into his arms and carrying her back towards the hotel, pausing briefly in the entrance, turning with a slight bow to acknowledge a chorus of cheers.

Once inside, however, Brodie dropped her to her feet, looking at her as if he didn't know quite what do with her.

Emmy, suddenly rather afraid that his tender concern was about to evaporate, hurriedly said, 'What about the car?' It was still slewed halfway out into the road, presumably with a sizeable dent in its rear.

'Girard is dealing with it. And he'll settle things with the other driver, too.' He regarded her with exasperation. 'You're running up quite a bill, Emmy. I hope you think your artist is worth it.' He didn't wait for her reply but turned and headed for the stairs. She began to follow him but he turned and blocked her way. 'Stay here, Emmy.'

'Why? What are you going to do?'

'Nothing.' There was a muscle working overtime at his jaw, she noticed. He was a man holding himself very firmly in check. 'Absolutely nothing if you stay here and behave yourself while I get dressed. I'll be ten minutes, no more, and then we'll go and find somewhere to eat.'

'But — '

'Don't argue with me. Just do as

you're told for once, because next time you try a stunt like that I promise you won't get off so lightly.' She was right. The concern had burned out in the heat of that kiss. Well, it had been worth it. But she wasn't about to let him see that, so she glared up at him.

'What will you do, Brodie?' she challenged, arms akimbo, as beneath his scorn she forgot all about being sorry for causing so much bother. 'Put me over your knee?'

'Something like that,' he said tightly. Then repeated the words. 'Something like that.'

Like? *Like?* What the heck did that mean? And then with a little shiver she realised exactly what he meant. When he had referred to her 'stunt' he hadn't been talking about her bid for escape, or the car accident. He had been referring to the way she had kissed him.

And, remembering exactly what had driven her to make a run for it, her poor cheeks heated up in a blush that would have jump-started the national grid.

★ ★ ★

Brodie had not been idly boasting about the extent of his wardrobe. When, rather less than ten minutes later, he returned to the hotel lobby he was dressed in a pair of lightweight chinos and a polo shirt in an uncommon shade of petrol-blue that did something curious to the shade of his eyes. In a more self-conscious man Emmy would have suspected that it was deliberate. In Brodie's case she had the depressing suspicion that it had been the choice of some woman, some incredibly glamorous, sophisticated woman who never gave him a moment of trouble and whose kisses were responded to with rather more enthusiasm. Although, come to think of it, his response had been extremely enthusiastic at the time . . . it was only on reflection that he had decided she had followed his instructions with rather too much enthusiasm. The thought served to cheer her slightly.

'You're still here, then,' he said, looking up from fastening his watch.

'I didn't have much choice.' She wiggled her bare toes. 'I left my shoes and bag in the car, and your tame hotelier has them tucked away some-where.'

'And you let a little thing like that stop you?' He regarded her with a certain wry amusement. 'You really mustn't let these minor set-backs dampen your determination, Emmy.'

'I won't,' she promised. 'But all the determination in the world won't get me beyond the end of the street without shoes.'

He retrieved her possessions from the girl behind the reception desk and handed them to her. 'All you had to do was ask.'

She made no attempt to disguise her disbelief. 'You really expect me to believe that?'

He shrugged. 'It was worth a try. Now you'll never know whether you'd have got away with it.'

'There's about as much chance of pigs flying,' she retorted irritably. 'Besides, I'm hungry.'

He smiled at that. 'If you want to eat I'm afraid you'll have to return the thousand francs you took from my wallet.'

She opened her bag and handed the money to him. 'It was only a loan. You would have been quite welcome to reimburse yourself from the money you took from me,' she informed him.

'I'll remember that, should the need ever arise.' He made it sound extremely unlikely. He waited while she slipped into her sandals. 'Ready?' She nodded, rising to her feet. He frowned. 'Sure? You still look a bit pale.'

Only because she spent so much time in his company blushing. 'I'm absolutely fine. Don't fuss.'

'I'm not fussing. If you hit your head in that shunt, just tell me. I don't want you passing out with concussion.' He *did* care, she thought happily, before he spoilt the effect by adding, 'I'd never be able to explain it to your father.'

For a moment she was tempted to consign her father, and Brodie with him, to the devil. But she couldn't stay cross with Brodie for more than two minutes together, and instead she giggled. 'It would almost be worth it to see you try,' she said. Then she slipped her hand through his arm. 'Come on, Brodie. Let's have a look at this sunset you've been promising me. I warn you, it had better be good.'

The sunset was brief but spectacular, colouring the sky in a kaleidoscope of reds and pinks and purples that provided a brilliant backdrop to the city and the harbour with its forest of bobbing masts belonging to all kinds of crafts, from huge luxury yachts to the more workaday fishing boats.

'Well,' Brodie asked as he settled her at a restaurant table on a terrace overlooking the harbour. 'Did it live up to its billing?'

'Not bad,' she said. 'A bit flashy for my taste. I prefer the silver and pink ones with the little bubbly clouds.'

'I'm afraid there is a cloud shortage in this part of the world right now, and frankly I hope it stays that way. Storms in this area tend to be rather like the sunsets.' Emmy lifted a querying brow. 'Spectacular with a definite leaning towards flashy,' he said.

'You seem to know your way about around here.'

'Yes, well, I worked as a deckhand on a yacht based here for a couple of summers. While I was at university.'

'Lucky you. After the unfortunate affair with Oliver Hayward I was condemned to spend all my long vacations trailing around museums in the company of an aunt.'

'Poor lady,' he said, with feeling. 'She has my sympathy.'

'No, I was good.' She flickered a glance in his direction. 'Honestly, Brodie. She would have been so distressed if I'd done anything scandalous . . . Besides, the Victoria and Albert Museum has a very sobering effect on me,' she added seriously.

'I wish you'd told me that before we left London; I'd willingly have sacrificed half a day in the interests of dampening your sudden urges to bolt. But I'm sure I could work up a fairly convincing degree of distress if it would encourage you to behave,' he offered.

'Could you?' She smiled absently. 'No, Aunt Louise felt so utterly responsible, I just couldn't upset her. She's a perfect love.'

'And I am not?' He grinned. 'Don't worry, you can say it. You won't hurt my feelings.'

'You are not in the least bit like my aunt Louise,' she said, carefully.

'And, besides, you had the whole of term-time in Oxford in which to get up to all the mischief in the world.'

'That's true.' She regarded him evenly. 'I also managed to cram in a first-class honours degree. It was a busy three years.'

He stared at her for a moment and then he shook his head. 'I'm sorry,

Emmy. I was being extremely rude — '

'Yes, you were.' Then she reached across and laid her hand on his. 'But there's no need to apologise. I've given you a rotten time and you've been wonderful. I don't know what I would have done about that man who ran into me if you hadn't been there.'

'Yes, you do.' He ignored the fact that if he hadn't been there she wouldn't have felt the need to make a dash for it. But, no matter how sweetly her hand lay on his, he wasn't about to let her think she was kidding him. 'You'd have batted your eyelashes at him and had him at your feet in ten seconds flat.'

'That's a perfectly horrible thing to say!' she protested, jerking back her hand.

'Is it? You forget I've had first-hand experience of the technique — when you were swinging from that drainpipe. And then you have a very interesting technique with stockings — '

'I did not bat my eyelashes! I was far too desperate to think of it at the time, and I had to put on my stockings or my shoes would have rubbed. Anyway, it's perfectly obvious that you're not at my feet, Brodie.'

He wasn't so sure about that, but it would undoubtedly be a mistake to tell her so. The slightest sign of weakness and she'd be twisting him around her little finger.

'No, well, I seem to spend all my time chasing after you. Even when you've promised to be good. I can't do that if I'm on my knees.' The waiter was hovering and, glad of the distraction, Brodie asked Emmy what she would like to drink.

'St Raphael, white, please,' she replied.

'And a Ricard for me,' he added, taking the menu. 'So, if it's not to be bouillabaisse, Emmy, what would you like to eat?'

'Grilled *rougets*, and a *mesclun*, please.'

'Wouldn't you prefer to look at the menu before you decide?'

179

'No.' She smiled, propping her elbows on the table and her chin in the palms of her hands. 'I know what I want.' He turned and asked the waiter if it was possible to have simple grilled *rougets* with a leaf salad. The waiter, eyes fixed on Emmy, assured him that it could be done.

'Do you always get what you want that easily?' he asked, once he had given the man his order.

'Not always. I didn't get Oliver Hayward. And if you and my father get your way I won't get Kit.'

'Oliver Hayward? He's the guy your father bought off when you were eighteen? Are you still mad at him about that?'

'No, I have to admit that Oliver was a mistake,' she told him. She gave a little shrug, embellished it with a tiny smile. 'I met him on that really long holiday you get between A-levels and university. I was staying with friends in Italy for the summer and so was he. Long, golden days with nothing to do except

180

eat, drink, swim and fall in love. And Oliver was terribly easy to fall in love with. He was as pretty as a picture, a charmer of the first water, the kind of man that mothers warn their daughters about.'

She pulled a face. 'Unfortunately my mother was always so busy having affairs with men exactly like him that she never got around to it. I suppose I should be grateful that he took my father's money. It showed him up for what he was.' She leaned back and linked her hands behind her head. 'He was very apologetic about it. Assured me that he was heartbroken, but he could see my father was serious about stopping the wedding whatever it took. He said he didn't want to make life difficult for me.'

'For *you*?'

'Hmm. Thoughtful, huh?' She grinned, broadly, dispelling any thoughts that she might be harbouring a lingering passion. 'And he managed to console himself with a new car.'

'Were you really in love with him, Emmy?'

'Or just winding up my beloved papa? Not guilty, Brodie. I've never had to work at it that hard. All I was guilty of was being eighteen years old and madly impressionable.' She shrugged. 'Then I was just mad. At Dad *and* Oliver. Dear God, the man could at least have held out for more . . . to have taken Hollingworth's first offer suggested a certain lack of . . . '

'Commitment?' Brodie offered, when she hesitated.

'The word I had in mind was guts.'

'Maybe he just had a particularly firm grasp of reality. Maybe, once someone had offered him the choice, he weighed the advantages of a hundred thousand pounds in the bank against the responsibilities of marriage and realised that he needed a new car more than he needed a wife. Particularly one who was likely to cause him a whole lot of bother.' He paused. 'What is Kit Fairfax driving, by the way?'

She lowered her lashes. 'That was below the belt, Brodie.'

'Just a thought.'

'Well, think about something else. As far as this conversation goes, Kit is off-limits.'

'Whatever you say.' He leaned back and, taking a swallow of his drink, regarded the harbour. 'It's odd, though. In my experience women usually find it impossible to stop talking about the man they are in love with.'

'I am not most women.'

He glanced briefly at her. 'That has not escaped my notice.' Then he gestured to the scene in front of them. 'Which of those boats do you wish you were on right now?' She regarded him distrustfully. 'I'm changing the subject, as requested, Emmy,' he said, quite gently.

'Oh.' She glanced at the harbour, then pulled a face. 'I sail in nothing smaller than the QE2. I get seasick.'

'You do have a bad time travelling, don't you? Frightened of planes, sick in boats . . . Now, me, I'd like to be aboard that big job over there, setting out for the Aegean, cruising around all those lovely islands, poking about the ruins, picnicking on the beach, sunbathing.'

'Is that what you used to do? When you were a deckhand?'

He gave her an old-fashioned look. 'No, Emmy. That's what the people who chartered the boats did. I fetched and carried and cleaned up after them.'

'Did you enjoy it?'

'Not all of it. But I had the sun and the chance to swim whenever I had an hour to spare. And some of the people who chartered the boats were really kind.'

'The women, you mean,' she said, cynically.

He laughed, revealing a full set of white, even teeth. 'Maybe I do. I can assure you that it beat the hell out of stacking shelves in a supermarket. And I didn't have to pay rent.'

She looked at him for a moment,

then said, 'You must think I'm very stupid.' She stared down into her glass. 'Over-privileged and thoughtless and very stupid.'

'No, I don't think that. We come from different worlds, that's all. I've had to work for everything I've ever had. But that's okay. The harder you work for something, the more you appreciate it.'

She thought about his amazing apartment, the pictures he had collected. Everything by the sweat of his brow, unlike her own flat, filled with hand-me-down antiques. Even the flat was a hand-me-down, inherited, along with her wealth, from her grandmother.

'Where do you come from, Brodie? What kind of people?' He didn't answer straight away, and once more she reached across the table as if to touch his arm, then apparently thought better of it and withdrew. 'I'd really like to know.'

He shrugged. 'My father was a miner. He was a big man, full of life. He loved to play cricket — he was good too. And he liked to walk — anything, really, to be out of doors breathing good, fresh air.'

'What happened to him?'

'He was killed in an accident underground when I was twelve. A machine . . . ' He caught himself. What the machine had done to his father was not a fit subject for polite conversation. 'I'd just been picked for the school cricket team. The youngest boy ever. He'd spent hours coaching me and he was so proud . . . '

'He never saw you play?' He shook his head. 'Life's a bitch, isn't it?' she said, and it suddenly occurred to Brodie that being abandoned by your mother as an infant couldn't have been a great start in life, no matter how many silver spoons Nanny had to feed you with. 'Did your mother never remarry?' she asked.

'No, she always said that Dad was too big an act to follow. But once I was off her hands she went to live near her sister in Canada.'

'She must miss you terribly.'

'She doesn't have time. Meg, her sister, had half a dozen children and they're well into the second generation now. I'd have to start competing in the baby stakes to persuade her to come back.'

'Why don't you?'

'It requires two, Emmy.' He glanced at her. 'The right two.'

'You're a 'till death us do part' man, are you?'

'If you don't at least start with 'till death us do part' as your goal there doesn't seem to be a lot of point. Marriage is enough of a lottery without being handicapped by a lack of commitment.'

'I suppose so. I guess I had a lucky escape when Oliver chose the money.' Emmy glanced at Brodie and discovered that she, too, was the object of thoughtful contemplation. 'Oh, look, here comes our supper.' She smiled brilliantly at the young waiter and he blushed, and when she caught Brodie's eye again he was no longer regarding her thoughtfully, but with exasperation.

'Do you have to do that?' he demanded.

'What?'

He just shook his head. 'It's not kind, Emmy.' She continued to stare at him, eyes wide. 'Nor is that,' he said, suddenly angry.

7

Brodie sat back while the man served their food, taking the chance to regain mastery of a libido racketing out of control. What on earth was the girl playing at? Was it unconscious? Had she no idea of the effect she had on him? Or was she doing it deliberately to distract him, knowing damn well that he was in no position to respond to the signals she was flashing at him?

The way she had kissed him outside the hotel had been a no holds barred, one hundred per cent effort, and for a few giddy moments he had forgotten everything but the way she felt in his arms, the way they seemed to fit together like two halves of the same piece, how desperately easy she would be to love. Well, he had urged her to be convincing, so perhaps he'd deserved everything she'd thrown at him.

But any more convincing and he'd have found it hard to remember the reason they were in France, to have left her downstairs in the hotel lobby when the only thing on his mind had been a bed that seemed to be taking on vast proportions, filling their suite, filling his head with thoughts of Emerald Carlisle that had nothing to do with business and everything to do with pleasure.

His desire for her, fired the moment he had set eyes on her, had now settled into a permanent dull ache that made him feel too small for his skin, made him long to be able to tear off his clothes and jump into the harbour to cool off.

The situation was intolerable, and a sane man would be wishing himself anywhere but here. But he wasn't. He couldn't think of anywhere he would rather be. Which made the thought of what would happen tomorrow unbearable. Either way. Because, whilst he was determined to carry out Gerald Carlisle's instructions to the letter, he couldn't bear the thought of Emerald being hurt. Again. No matter how lightly she had brushed it off, rationalising it as a lucky escape, he knew that Oliver Hayward's faithlessness had hurt.

And he hated Gerald Carlisle for the kind of heavy-handedness that had made it inevitable. It had obviously been a holiday romance, the kind that flares and dies as quickly, leaving precious, bittersweet memories, a few old photographs to be smiled over years later when the kids found them stuffed away in a box in the attic. Her father had destroyed all that.

'Tell me about your job, Emmy,' he said abruptly as the waiter reluctantly moved away. When she didn't say anything he looked up. She was regarding him with a slightly puzzled expression, rather like a puppy who has been yelled at but has no idea why. He wanted to wrap her in his arms, kiss her, reassure her that everything would be fine. But he couldn't do that. There were no guarantees, even if he knew exactly what she wanted. All he really knew was that she was determined to get to Kit Fairfax before him.

'Please,' he added, aware that he had been curt, that as his throat had tightened with longing his words had come out like an order rather than a conversational gambit.

She continued to look at him for another thirty seconds before she finally lowered her eyes and picked up her fork. 'I told you, I'm a trainee at Aston's, the auctioneers. I'm doing the rounds at the moment — you know, three months in each department.' She toyed with her fish. 'But I want to specialise in toys and automata. Mechanical toys,' she explained uncertainly.

'Little singing birds in cages, that sort of thing?'

She laughed, breaking the tension. 'That sort of thing,' she agreed. 'And a whole lot more. Some are wonderfully elaborate groups of figures — beautifully dressed musicians, clowns, beggars even. They were always rare and prized.' She pulled a tiny moue. 'Rich men's toys, Brodie. They cost a fortune even when they were first made. The very finest ones were made here in France.'

'Really? I didn't know that. Do you collect them?'

She gave him an odd look. 'Do you really think that Hollingworth would let me loose with that kind of money?'

'I couldn't say. He doesn't discuss his clients' business with me unless he wants a legal opinion. Your petty cash hardly comes into that category, Miss Carlisle.'

'Hardly petty cash, Brodie. But it's academic anyway. I believe the best pieces should be in public collections where they can be properly cared for and everyone can enjoy them. Too much wonderful stuff is locked away, never looked at until it has appreciated in value sufficiently to be auctioned on to someone else who'll probably do exactly the same with it.' She was positively glowing with fervour, her red curls shining like a halo under the lights. 'It's such a waste.'

'You could buy one and donate it to the V and A,' he suggested. 'Maybe it would make the place less sobering . . . '

'The Victoria and Albert Museum, Brodie, is sobering in the right kind of way. It makes you stop and think. All that work, the skill, the dedication of centuries of craftsmen, some of them working for just pennies to make useful things as beautiful as the heart could aspire to, things that the people who made them could never afford to have themselves . . . ' She trailed off, slightly embarrassed. 'Actually I did buy a little automaton a few months ago. It's just a moth-eaten little monkey with some cymbals, with a very simple movement. It needs some work but a craftsman I know is going to help me to restore it.'

This was safer ground, for both of them. 'How do you go about that?' Brodie prompted. But she needed little encouragement as her enthusiasm for her subject carried her away. Describing the mechanical figures she had seen, amazing finds unearthed in barns, the fabulous prices some had made at auction, carried them easily on through fish and a melt-on-the-tongue apple tarte, to coffee and cognac.

'I'm sorry; I just get carried away once I start,' she said eventually. 'I've bored you rigid.'

Recalling the animated manner in which she had described her job, her enthusiasm, her obvious love for her work, he shook his head. 'You don't know how to be boring, Emmy.'

'Was that a compliment?' she enquired, so doubtfully that Brodie laughed out loud.

'Now you're just fishing. Come on, I think it's time we went back to the hotel. You've a big day ahead of you tomorrow, and I'd like to make an early start.'

'You're a glutton for punishment, Brodie. Don't you ever just turn over and lie in for half an hour?'

Yesterday his response would have been to offer to lie in all morning if she was prepared to join him. But flirting with her was no longer an option for him. He wanted her too much.

'You've clearly never slept on a sofa,' he said, taking care to keep his voice expressionless.

She had, but not in circumstances she was willing to discuss. 'I'd offer to swop, but you'd undoubtedly think I was planning to tiptoe out and make a run for it the moment you were asleep,' she said.

'Now, why on earth would I think a thing like that?' he enquired gently.

'But then again,' she continued, ignoring his question, 'you did make the reservations, so presumably you knew what to expect.'

'I wish. Come on, let's go and look at the boats.' She looked doubtful. 'Don't worry, I'm not planning to shanghai you.'

'Shanghai me?'

'Slip you a Mickey and whisk you

aboard while you are senseless.' She still looked puzzled. 'Don't you ever watch old movies?' he asked. She shook her head. 'You don't know what you're missing. A Mickey Finn,' he explained, 'is something slipped into a drink to knock you out. Once you're unconscious you get smuggled aboard some boat that's just leaving harbour, and by the time you wake up you're miles out to sea.'

'But why?'

'In your case to whisk you out of harm's way.'

'Kit would never harm me,' she said, her eyes pure gold in the reflected light. 'Unlike your friend Mickey,' she added solemnly. Then a dimple appeared at the corner of her mouth. He wanted to kiss it so badly that it was like an ache.

He probed at it, like a man worrying a bad tooth, taking her hand in his to cross the road. Her fingers were long and slender, the bones seeming impossibly fragile beneath his broad palm, stirring in him a desperate longing to protect her. What was it about this girl? She made him feel like a boy, awkward, foolish with his spiralling need for her.

She wasn't the first woman who'd turned his head. No man could reach thirty-one without making a fool of himself more than once. But she was the first woman he'd ached to love and yet whose desires and needs he knew he would always put above his own.

Tomorrow he was very afraid that he would lose her. But if Kit Fairfax was strong, if he was the man she wanted, he knew he would do everything in his power to help them. Was that the difference between lust and love?

But for the moment he retained his grasp on her hand as they wandered back towards their hotel along the edge of the harbour, and she seemed perfectly content to leave her fingers curled about his.

It was one of those perfect, bitter-sweet moments to store up against an empty future, he thought as his hand pressed against the small, hard circle of gold that she wore on the third finger of her left hand, the tiny diamond that Kit Fairfax had given her as a token of his love. She'd been fiddling with it unconsciously all evening, as if clinging to what it represented. Brodie punished himself with that thought. But he didn't let go of her hand.

'Is that the boat you would like to be on?' Emerald asked, stopping to point to one of the larger yachts.

He dragged his mind back to the harbour and less dangerous thoughts. 'Yes, that's her. Not exactly the QE2,' he observed, turning to lean on the rail, tucking her hand beneath his arm. 'But she's quite a beauty.'

'Yes, she's lovely. Perhaps in the right company I wouldn't notice the motion.' She turned to look up at him. 'Tell me, Brodie, if you could sail away right now where would you go?'

He thought for a moment, staring out across the harbour, listening to the rattle of the rigging as the yachts rose and fell on the water, remembering sun-filled days when he'd still had everything to prove. He'd proved it. Worked his way out of a pit village until he was standing in the South of France with an heiress on his arm. But he was suddenly faced with the realisation that unless she was his none of it meant anything. She was still looking at him, waiting for an answer. Where would he go?

'The isles of Greece, the isles of Greece!
Where burning Sappho loved and sung,
Where grew the arts of war and peace,
Where Delos rose, and Phoebus sprung!
Eternal summer gilds them yet,
But all, except their sun, is set.'

Brodie quoted the words softly, yet with such an intensity of feeling that Emmy suspected his real reason for working as a deckhand had owed more to some romantic schoolboy notion to visit the magical isles of Greece than any disinclination to stack supermarket shelves. Beneath that lawyer's stern exterior there beat the heart of a poet, an adventurer.

But then she had known that the moment she'd set eyes on him. And he had confirmed it by not betraying her. Lord, how she hated what she was doing to him! One more day. Just one more day . . .

It took every ounce of determination to instil a teasing note into her voice. 'I ask for an itinerary and I get Byron,' she said, with forced lightness. '*Don Juan*, no less. You're not exactly boring yourself, Brodie.' Then a yawn caught her by surprise.

'Not boring, huh?'

Her face, illuminated softly by the lights of the boats and the reflections off the water, filled with sudden laughter. 'No, Brodie,' she said. 'Whatever else you could say about today, it was certainly not boring.' She stretched up on her toes and kissed his cheek. 'Thank you for being so kind about the car.'

Kind? She left him bereft of words. What had she expected him to do? Shout at her? Shake her? He loved her, for heaven's sake. Loved her. In twenty-four hours she had swept into his life and turned it upside down. And he knew without the slightest doubt that he would gladly die for her.

Yet tomorrow he had to do everything in his power to persuade a man she thought she was in love with not to marry her. If he succeeded would she think him kind then?

Or was she simply trying to disarm him?

He resisted the temptation to turn his head, shift the kiss to her mouth. Instead, he lifted her hand to his lips and kissed the tips of her fingers.

'Just don't do it again,' he said thickly, turning her towards the hotel.

'No. No, I won't.' They walked on for a moment. 'Brodie?'

'Mmm.'

'Tomorrow, will you let me talk to Kit first? Just for a few minutes?'

He glanced down at her, but she was looking straight ahead, avoiding his eyes. He guessed that answered his question. 'No, Emmy,' he said, his heart like lead in his chest. 'If he loves you, you've got nothing to worry about.'

* * *

Emerald, lying tucked up in the huge bed all by herself, lay awake and worried. She simply had to speak to Kit before Brodie started on him or all her plans would just come crashing down around her ears.

She fiddled with the ring she was wearing. The wretched thing didn't fit properly and she had to keep bending her finger to stop it from slipping off. Well, one more day and she could take it off, and good riddance, but first she had to get to Kit, explain the situation to him before Brodie turned on the pressure. And this time there must be no mistakes. She needed a proper plan rather than making a grab for freedom when a chance presented itself. She'd tried that three times and it hadn't got her anywhere.

Well, actually, taking her chances had got her as far as France. If she hadn't taken the chances when they had been offered she would still be mouldering at Honeybourne.

And taking her chances had got her Brodie. Emmy's smooth brow puckered momentarily into a frown. Brodie was very special, a strong man who didn't use his strength to bully her like her father.

She could hear him moving about the other room, as wakeful as she was. What was he doing? Just pacing about, unable to sleep on that wretched sofa? It was the second night he'd been forced to surrender his bed to her. She was six inches shorter than him and fifty pounds lighter. The least she could do was offer, sincerely this time, to change places with him.

She eased herself out of bed, padded across the darkened room and opened the door a few inches. Brodie had come to rest in a large armchair on the far side of the room. He was wearing the thin track-suit bottoms but hadn't bothered with a T-shirt, and the golden light from a lamp on the table behind him pooled on the silken skin of his shoulders, throwing the sculptured lines of his chest into sharp relief, hinting at the darker cruciform shadow of body hair.

He was so beautiful that her heart clenched with longing to throw open the door and run to him, fling her arms about his knees, beg him to sail away with her to his wonderful islands. If he would just look up so that she could see his eyes, see them unguarded as he suddenly noticed her. Then she saw the open file on his knees. He wasn't about to look up; he was too absorbed in Mark Reed's file to be aware of her presence, too busy trying to work out what kind of man Kit Fairfax was and just how likely he was to take the money and run.

A mixture of emotions boiled up in her. Resentment, mostly, but with an undertow of something raw and painful. Brodie was supposed to be her knight in shining armour. He was. Or rather he had been. But tomorrow would be different.

And if tomorrow was going to produce the results she wanted she had better start thinking instead of dreaming.

She closed the door and climbed back into bed.

So far she had relied on chance, taken her opportunities as they had presented themselves. But now she would have to make things happen. She needed a plan.

It didn't take a lot of devising; she didn't have a lot of choices open to her, or much time. She abandoned any thought of trying to creep past him while he was asleep. The risk was too great, and if she failed, he would make certain she didn't have another chance.

No, she would wait until Brodie was taking a shower in the morning. He was sure to let her use the bathroom first. Then, once he was at his own ablutions, she would have a few moments in which to escape. She'd only take her handbag, leaving her overnight case, her make-up on the dressing table, so that he wouldn't be immediately suspicious.

Maybe she should leave her handbag, too? All she really needed was the five hundred francs she had hidden from him. And a handkerchief. And a lipstick. Her little diary with directions to the farmhouse. Nothing that wouldn't slip into the pockets of her jeans.

If only she could have been sure she had enough money for a taxi, but she didn't know how far the village was from Aix. How far the farmhouse was from the village. Kit had been terribly vague about distances; extracting the directions from him had been difficult enough when he'd been absorbed in his work.

She wished she had taken a closer look at that street map of Marseilles downstairs in the hotel reception, taken more notice of the buses and where they stopped. But the truth of the matter was that she hadn't been taking notice of anything except Brodie.

'*Où est l'arrêt d'autobus pour Aix, s'il vous plaît?*' she murmured half a dozen times or so, until the phrase rolled off her tongue without difficulty.

Satisfied, she slipped down beneath the cover and closed her eyes. The question was no problem. All she had to worry about now was whether she would understand the answer.

* * *

'Emmy? Are you awake?' She groaned. To anyone with half a brain it was perfectly obvious that she was fast asleep. The man was obsessed with getting up at the crack of dawn, and not even the smell of fresh coffee could redeem him this time. 'It's nearly eight-thirty,' he added.

Her lids flickered open. *Eight-thirty?* Could she have possibly heard that right? She eased herself into a sitting position, pushing her hair back from her eyes, and blinked sleepily. It had been a long time before she had slept last night. 'It can't be,' she said.

'I'm sorry. I left you as long as I could, but I do want to get this over with. I'm sure you do too.'

She groaned again. Kit. Her neat little escape plan all blown out of the window because she had overslept. Brodie, showered, shaved, dressed and ready to go, sat on the edge of the bed and handed her a cup of coffee.

'Here, this will help,' he said.

He was wrong, nothing would help, but she took it and sipped it anyway. 'Thank you.'

'Any time. There are some fresh croissants in the other room whenever you're ready.'

Coffee, croissants — room service? 'I thought we were supposed to eat those out on the pavement in the sun, watching the world go by?'

'Maybe tomorrow,' he said vaguely.

'Tomorrow?'

'You with Kit, perhaps. Me on some pavement café somewhere. Wherever the mood takes me.'

She gave him an old-fashioned look. 'Not if you can help it.'

'It's not what I'd prefer,' he agreed. 'But we have a deal. If your artist is the kind of man that money can't buy, I'll leave the field.' Then, 'Honestly,' he said, with the faintest of smiles. And it was then she noticed a slight greyness around his mouth, a heaviness to his lids. She was not the only one who had had difficulty sleeping last night.

'I believe you,' she said, putting out an impetuous hand, but he moved before she could touch him, stood up, and, remembering his accusation that she was not kind, she thought she understood why. *Oh, Brodie!* she thought, wistfully. *Hold on. Just hold on*.

'I cannot, however, guarantee your father's reaction,' he continued. 'If you stay in France he'll have a month in which to regroup. I've no doubt he'll summon Hollingworth from Scotland. Maybe he'll even call on your aunt Louise.'

'Maybe he'll ask you to shanghai me,' she offered. Not that she'd need a Mickey Finn to persuade her to sail away with Brodie into the sunset. Well, maybe just to get aboard. Once at sea she was sure he would distract her from any inclination towards *mal de mer*.

Her attempt at levity, however, was not appreciated.

'He could ask,' Brodie said, stiffly, 'but as his lawyer I'd have to inform him that it would be a criminal offence.' Then, slightly exasperated with her, 'You're an adult, Emmy, you can marry any number of fortune-hunters if you want to.'

'Always provided I remember to keep

to one fortune-hunter at a time,' she said, dryly.

'Maybe you should try telling your father that.' He paused, but only to gather breath. 'And, while you're telling him maybe you should ask him whether your happiness is less important than preserving a bank full of money that your family has been handing down since time immemorial, each succeeding generation increasingly nervous that someone might cheat them out of it.'

His concern cloaked her in warmth. But it was more than just concern. There was real feeling in his eyes, in his voice. And something more. Something she suspected he would not wish her to see. She wanted so much to reach up, put her arms about him and pull him down beside her, forget about the outside world. She only hoped that when this was all over he would be able to forgive her deception. That his eyes would still burn when he looked at her.

'My father isn't bad, Brodie. He just

worries about me. Probably with good reason,' she admitted. 'He's afraid I might turn out like my mother.'

'Then he's a bigger fool than I thought.'

He took the empty cup from her. He would have liked to add that it was his sincere wish that Fairfax would send Gerald Carlisle a message that would leave the man in no doubt as to what he should do with his money. But he couldn't bring himself to frame a sentiment that wasn't true. He wanted Kit Fairfax to be a snivelling, miserable reprobate who'd snatch his hand off. Unfortunately, he didn't think that likely. He didn't think Emmy was the kind of girl to make the same mistake twice.

'Quick as you can, Emmy,' he urged, although why he should have to urge her to hurry to her own wedding he wasn't quite certain. It wasn't something he wanted to think about.

★ ★ ★

Emmy waited until the door closed behind him. Then she rocketed out of bed, already adjusting her plan to meet the unexpected changes thrust on her by Brodie's thoughtfulness in letting her sleep on.

She rushed into the bathroom, turning on the shower full blast, leaving it to run while she retrieved her few basic essentials from her handbag and stuffed them into her jeans pocket while she had the chance. Then she took her time about showering and dressing in jeans and a white T-shirt, the kind of clothes everyone was wearing and would not be immediately noticeable, or memorable. And she took ages putting on the minimum of make-up. Brodie was impatient to be off. The more impatient he got, the more chance she had of succeeding.

She was zipping up her bag when Brodie finally knocked. 'How're you doing in there, Emmy?'

'I'm all ready.' She opened the door and handed him her overnight bag. 'But starving.' She tossed her handbag onto an armchair and headed for the croissants. 'Is there any more coffee?' she asked, settling herself on the sofa. Brodie poured her a cup, then picked up her bag. 'Oh, aren't you going to have one with me?'

'No. I'll go and pay the bill and put the bags in the car. It'll save time,' he said pointedly.

She smiled serenely, apparently oblivious to his urgency. 'Oh, right. Good idea.' She bit into the warm, buttery pastry. 'Mmm. These just don't taste the same when you buy them in London, do they?' she said, capturing a crumb with the tip of her finger and redirecting it towards her mouth. She was being quite deliberately provocative, sensing that it would drive him away more quickly than anything.

'I wouldn't know. I require rather more than a piece of pastry to see me through a working day.'

The minute the door closed behind him, she abandoned the croissant and crossed to the bathroom. She turned on the tap at the sink then carefully shut the bathroom door. She left the bedroom door open so that he would hear the water running and think she was in the bathroom. And she left her handbag on the chair where she had thrown it. Because every man knew that there wasn't a woman born who could manage without her handbag.

And then she let herself out of the bedroom and hurried towards the back stairs, startling a chambermaid with a pile of towels as she rounded a corner. '*Non, non, madame*,' the girl said, pointing to the main staircase as she rattled out a rapid stream of French. But Emmy, an imploring look in her eyes, put her finger to her lips and gestured towards the staff stairs. The girl's eyes widened, then Emmy saw understanding dawn. She pointed again to the back entrance of the hotel, and once more the girl launched into incomprehensible French.

The French might have been beyond

her, but it was obvious to Emmy that she had an ally — an ally, moreover, who would know the way to the bus stop. She repeated her carefully rehearsed question, but as she had feared the directions were too rapid, too complicated, and time was running out.

Emmy, the star of countless school plays, pointed dramatically to her watch and threw an anguished look in the direction of the main stairs. The girl, thrilled to be part of some romantic conspiracy, abandoned the towels on the hall table and led her by the back way from the hotel, dodging the kitchen staff, taking care that she was not seen.

She took her first down a narrow lane and then around a corner, where she stopped and pointed across the road to the bus stop. Emmy pressed one of her precious hundred-franc notes into the girl's hand. Her help had been worth every centime.

Ten minutes later she was on a bus headed towards Aix-en-Provence. It was, she knew, about twenty miles, half an hour by car, give or take a few minutes for traffic. By bus it would take longer, and she sincerely regretted telling Brodie which direction to take.

8

Brodie was feeling absolutely bloody. He hadn't slept; he hadn't even tried. Instead he'd spent the night going through the file Carlisle had given him, trying to put his finger on what it was that was bothering him about this whole business. Trying, he knew, to find some damning piece of information about Kit Fairfax, some lever to use to make him back off without having to offer him money, because if he took it Emmy would never trust another man. And Brodie wouldn't blame her.

But Mark Reed had found nothing about Kit Fairfax that he could use as an arm twister. No drugs, no wife in the attic, no horde of illegitimate children. He was just one more struggling artist.

He would have liked to see some of his pictures, get a feel for the man through his work, but there was nothing like that in the file to help him.

Emmy had visited him at his studio a couple of times a week. A couple of weeks ago she had stayed overnight. He forced himself to ignore the hot rush of jealousy that engulfed him. Jealousy would not help; emotion would simply cloud his judgement. He uncurled fingers that had tightened around the folder, and after a few moments he continued to scan Mark Reed's notes. Not that there was much to learn.

Emmy had always gone to Fairfax's studio; he had never been observed going to her flat. She'd stayed an hour or so on each occasion . . . his fingers tightened again . . . then sometimes they'd gone to the local pub for a drink and a sandwich then she had gone home or on to somewhere else with friends. Fairfax had gone back to his studio. That was all. He'd never called her at work, or sent her flowers or behaved in any way like a besotted lover. Scarcely the whirlwind romance that Emmy had presented her father with. Or maybe that was what Brodie wanted to believe.

Yet Gerald Carlisle must have had some reason to put Reed onto Fairfax. He bent to pick up a piece of paper that had slipped onto the floor. It was a cutting from one of those glossy country magazines. There was a picture of Emmy looking wonderfully glamorous at some charity auction. And the man she was looking at with every appearance of stars in her eyes was Kit Fairfax.

If he'd been asked to make a judgement, he would have said that Emmy had simply thrown herself at the man. And if the affair was so one-sided it was possible that Fairfax would be a push-over.

He stared up at the hotel window. One girl, two days, and his life would never be the same. Whatever happened.

But delaying things was not helping. He'd stowed the bags in the car, paid the bill and still Emmy hadn't appeared. He continued to stare up at the window, unwilling to return to their suite, wishing he had told her to come down when she was ready. But there was no point in putting the moment off any longer. He went back inside, mounting the stairs two at a time.

'Emmy, are you ready?' he called as he opened the door. 'Let's go,' he added, without waiting for an answer.

She wasn't in the sitting room. The bedroom door was open and as he approached it he heard the water running and shrugged. He returned to the sitting room, glancing around to make sure that nothing had been left behind.

There was nothing. Just her handbag on the chair. A croissant with one bite missing. The cup of coffee he'd poured her gone cold. He glanced back at the bedroom, anxiety clutching suddenly at his stomach. Was she sick? The change of water, different food . . .

'Emmy?' he called. 'Are you all right?' When she didn't reply he tapped at the bathroom door. 'Emmy?' He turned the handle, half opened the door.

And then in a flash he knew. He didn't need to see the water trickling from the tap into the sink, or to fling back the door on the empty bathroom to know what she had done.

He didn't stop to turn the water off. He didn't waste his breath on calling himself every kind of fool he could lay his tongue to. It might have made him feel marginally better for about ten seconds, but it wouldn't help him find Emerald Carlisle.

Hurtling through the door, Brodie practically bowled over the chambermaid. He grabbed her to steady her, full of apologies. Then as, blushing, she ducked away from him he turned back. She might have seen Emmy leave the hotel by the back way; it was certainly worth asking.

'*Excusez-moi, mademoiselle,*' he began. '*Avez vous . . . ?*' But she backed nervously away before he could even complete his question, jabbering nervously about how busy she was, how late it was, diving into the nearest bedroom in her anxiety to avoid him.

Such obvious panic at the thought of being asked the simplest of questions made him pause. He could have been about to ask if she had seen his car keys, or if she had some soap, or something as mundane as the time. But from her reaction it would appear she knew exactly what he had been about to ask her and that she had something to hide.

He followed her to the doorway. 'Which way did she go?' he asked in French, without further preliminaries. Then, 'Did you lend her money?' He took out his wallet, intending to repay her.

'*Non, non, monsieur!*' She shook her hands at him, holding him at a distance as he advanced upon her.

She was young and very nervous. Realising that he would get nowhere by scaring the girl, he explained patiently that he only wished to repay her. Dumbly now she shook her head, and took out a hundred-franc note to show him.

So, Emmy had had money all the time. He wondered how much. The one thing he didn't need to ask himself was where she'd kept it hidden. Clearly babysitting Emmy Carlisle was no job for a gentleman.

'Where was she going?' he asked, firmly but quietly. 'Tell me now, or I'll have to fetch Madame Girard.' The prospect of interrogation by that indomitable lady was too much for the girl and she began to weep.

Brodie raised his eyes to the ceiling. Heaven alone knew what Emmy had told her. Not much. Her French was not up to some elaborate tale of wife-beating or worse. Even supposing she'd had the time. But with a sigh, a gesture ... He'd experienced the technique firsthand and she'd reduced him to slavery with little more than a look. He handed the girl his handkerchief and waited, curtailing his impatience with difficulty, until her sobs had subsided. Then he set about convincing her that he intended Emerald no harm.

Placing his hands gently on her shoulders, he looked down at her. '*Mademoiselle*, she is in the gravest danger,' he said, with quiet urgency, disregarding the truth. The truth was that he hadn't the slightest idea what kind of danger Emmy had got herself into, if any, but until he did he wasn't going to let her off the hook. The girl's eyes widened. 'I have to find her before she does something foolish.' The girl continued to stare at him. 'I love her,' he declared in desperation, his hands tightening on the girl's shoulders. 'I love her.' He repeated the words in the manner of a man who had just discovered some hitherto unsuspected truth. 'I swear that I would never do anything to hurt her.'

Thirty seconds later he was reversing the car out of the parking bay and heading for Aix, while the young chambermaid was sitting on the bed she was supposed to be stripping, clutching a hundred-franc note in each hand, a big grin on her face, congratulating herself on having swopped shifts with her sister.

'Aix' wasn't much of a clue. But it was a start. Once there she would undoubtedly be heading out into the country for some cottage or converted farmhouse belonging to friends. She would only have to make a quick phone call once she'd reached the town and Fairfax would come and meet her. Then it would be like searching for a needle in a haystack. If he didn't find her first.

Halted at a junction blocked solid with traffic, he punched Mark Reed's number into his mobile phone. 'Mark? Tom Brodie. What have you got for me?'

'Not a lot. None of Miss Carlisle's friends seem to know where she was going, or if they do they're not telling. The only lead I've got is a postcard sent by Fairfax to his next-door neighbour, telling him that things were taking longer than he anticipated and asking him to continue feeding the cat until he comes home — '

'Things?'

'Your guess is as good as mine. The postmark is unreadable, but the picture is of a painting by Cézanne of a mountain — '

'*La Montagne Sainte Victoire?*'

'That's it. He said on the card that it was the view from his farmhouse window.'

'I know it. Unfortunately it's the view from half the region. But at least we're in the right area. All right, Mark, that's some help.'

'Given you the slip again, has she?' he said, not without sympathy. 'She's quite a girl for that. Ducking you in Harvey Nic's and then giving you a little wave when she gets home with her shopping. Just to let you know she knows you're there.'

'I'm considering handcuffs,' Brodie said, tight-lipped.

'Poor kid's been in handcuffs, meta-phorically speaking, ever since she was old enough to have a mind of her own. Carlisle should try trusting her for once; she's his daughter, not his wife.' He seemed to hesitate. 'She's a nice girl, Tom.'

'Yes.' The traffic began to edge forward. 'Tell me, you've seen them together, would you say she's in love with Fairfax?'

'I couldn't say. She always seemed flirtatious around him, but, as I said, she knew she was being watched. It could all have been a bit of a game to tease her father, if you know what I mean.'

'Yes, I know exactly what you mean,' he said, with considerable feeling. She liked to tease.

'She's done it before, you see. Once she cottoned on to the fact that he checked up on her boyfriends. She moved into a flat with one of them once and the Honourable Gerald was fit to be tied. In fact the bloke had gone away and she was just looking after his plants. At least that's what she said,

229

when he went charging around there, as if butter wouldn't melt in her mouth.'

'Is that right? Well, if her friends are being cagey, why don't you try the diary editors? They can't resist showing off just how much they know about what's going on. It's getting urgent, Mark.' Another couple of hours and she would have won.

The traffic began to move and gradually he edged free of the town centre traffic and headed for Aix. He caught up with the bus after half a dozen miles or so.

A bus, he reminded himself; it might not be the right bus. And the possibility that the chambermaid might have been lying to protect Emmy had not escaped him, although she had been in such a state of confusion that it seemed unlikely. But Emmy must have anticipated he would question the staff, and she was quite capable of laying a false trail. He was beginning to think she was capable of anything.

Hadn't she escaped from a second-floor room at Honeybourne, stowed away in his car, then stolen it the moment the opportunity had presented itself? She had never ceased trying to evade him, trying to get to Kit Fairfax before he could talk to him.

Why? What did she have to tell the man that would make such a difference to the outcome? Whatever it was, she clearly wasn't convinced that love would be enough to hold him steadfast.

It was that belief that drove him on. There was, after all, no imminent danger of the marriage taking place. But there was *something* . . . and he refused to be beaten by a leggy girl, even if he was crazy about her.

He tucked in a few cars behind the bus and mentally crossed his fingers, hoping that Miss Emerald Carlisle hadn't had time for anything as complicated as laying false trails.

No. There was Kit's postcard. He frowned, picked up the mobile lying on the seat beside him and pressed redial.

'Mark? Tom Brodie, again. Did Fairfax say *his* farmhouse on that postcard?'

'I think so. Hold on a minute, I wrote it down.' There was a pause while he consulted his notebook. 'Yes, that's what he said; 'my farmhouse'. Ah, I think I see what you're getting at. I'll ring you back.'

* * *

Emmy had chosen to sit in the centre of the bus on an aisle seat. The last thing she needed was Brodie cruising past in his car and spotting her carrot-coloured mop of hair. It stood out like a beacon amongst the dark-haired locals. She should have worn a hat, or a scarf. Except she hadn't packed one. There was no way she could have anticipated that she would be hiding out on a bus . . .

She leaned forward to see past the plump matron who occupied the window seat. Cars sped by, but there was no sign of Brodie. She tried to recall exactly what she had said to him. North and then east. Would he be able to work it out? In time?

She turned the other way and glanced behind. There was a stream of traffic, any number of dark-coloured Renaults. But this was France; what did she expect? As she straightened a young man in the seat opposite smiled at her. She smiled back automatically.

They were coming into a village, and the bus pulled over. The woman beside her made a move to get out and Emmy stood up to let her by. It was at that moment, as the cars behind swooshed past, that she found herself looking straight down out of the back of the bus into Brodie's face. For a moment she froze, unable to decide whether to stay put, run for it, or simply surrender.

The bus moving forward, throwing her sideways, made up her mind for her. She lowered herself onto her seat and tried to think. Tried not to look behind her. He had been so quick! Whatever had he done to that poor chambermaid to get her to tell? She grinned. Smiled at her. That was all it would have taken. But even so. To get so quickly on her trail . . .

But then, what had she expected? It was his quick wits that had so delighted her when he'd allowed her to escape from Honeybourne in the first place. But since then he had matched her every step of the way, countering every move she made with a persistence that was driving her to the point of desperation.

The bus had seemed for the briefest space of time to be her salvation. Now she was trapped on it. The moment she stepped off it he would be there, and this time there was the distinct possibility that he wouldn't be as kind as he had been when she had reversed into that car.

She would thank him for that, properly, when all this was over. The briefest of smiles crossed her lips as she paused momentarily to dwell on the pleasures to come. But for now the most important thing was to get away from him. An hour, that was all she needed . . .

In the front of the bus the driver was using a radio, or telephone, to talk to his control centre, and Emerald gave a little gasp as an idea came to her.

She immediately rejected it. No. No, she couldn't do that. It would be too dreadful . . . Brodie would never forgive her . . . But there was Kit to think of . . .

She got up, made her way to the front of the bus. '*Pardon,*' she began, hesitantly. The bus driver glanced at her. '*Parlez-vous anglais?*' The driver shook his head. Aware that all the other passengers were straining to hear, she turned to appeal to them. 'Please,' she said. 'I'm being followed by a strange man. He stole that car.' She pointed to the rear of the bus. Two dozen pairs of eyes glanced behind and then turned to regard her expectantly. '*Un stalker!*' she tried, a little desperately. They were getting close to Aix. '*Un stalker anglais!'* She picked up the driver's telephone. *'Appelez les gendarmes!'* she declared dramatically.

As the driver, urged on by his excited passengers, summoned assistance on her behalf, Emmy collapsed back into her seat, vowing that she would enrol for French lessons the moment she got home.

* * *

Brodie wasn't sure what Emmy thought she could accomplish by staying on the bus. She would have been more comfortable getting off and joining him in the car. Yet at each stop she seemed to make a point of showing him that she was not getting off, turning to look at him with those luminous eyes as he waited patiently for the passengers to alight and the journey to continue. It made him uneasy. But what could she do on a bus?

On the outskirts of Aix he discovered exactly what Emerald Carlisle was capable of as two police cars, lights flashing, moved in on him, one swerving in front of him forcing him to a halt, the second closing up behind him.

Brodie switched off the engine of the Renault and climbed out of the car, holding his hands clearly in sight as the *Gendarmes* descended upon him, but he wasn't looking at them. He was watching the bus pull away from him. And Emmy looking back at him. She mouthed something. Could it have been 'Sorry'? He rather thought it had been.

But he was in no hurry to forgive her for this. In fact at that moment he sincerely regretted not having called the police when Emerald Carlisle had stolen his car. He could so easily have told her father that he hadn't known he had Emmy on board. She wouldn't have betrayed him.

A few hours in a police cell might have made her think again about the advisability of runaway weddings. And she would have been handed straight back to her father. He was beginning to sympathise with the man.

No. Sympathising with Gerald Carlisle was going too far.

But as his hands were fastened none too gently in handcuffs and he was bundled into a police car he wondered just what she had been finally driven to. What had she accused him of to bring the police down on his head at breakneck speed? Nothing trivial, he could be certain of that. And unlike an angry driver with a dent in his front wing, the French *gendarmerie* would not be soothed by a few thousand francs.

★ ★ ★

Emmy stared out of the bus window as the police cut Brodie out of the traffic and brought him dramatically to a halt. Everyone on the bus cheered and smiled at her approvingly.

She felt truly terrible. Terrible for

what she had done to Brodie. Terrible for deceiving these kind people. She shouldn't have done it. She should stop it now, but as she rose to her feet the bus accelerated away from the scene. She stood, clutching the back of her seat, her heart doing ridiculous, impossible things, one moment in her throat, the next in her boots as she saw the *Gendarmes* advance on Brodie, saw him climb from the car, saw him staring after her. She mouthed a desperate 'sorry', but it was too late.

The moment she arrived in Aix she would go straight to the local police, explain to them what she had done. Then they would have to let him go. She subsided into her seat, oblivious to the excited chatter around her.

But suppose they let him go and kept her in custody for wasting police time? He would still be angry with her, maybe so angry that he would leave her there in the police station until he had found Kit and discovered exactly what she had been planning. Maybe he wouldn't even do that. Maybe he would just go straight back to England and leave her locked up until Hollingworth was despatched to extricate her from yet another mess. She wouldn't blame him. She wouldn't blame him one bit. But she couldn't take that risk.

No. What was done was done. She would wait until she got to the village near Kit's farmhouse and *then* she would telephone the police, or it would all have been a waste and Brodie would have been arrested to no avail.

At least this way his suffering would have some point. She knew he would come after her, if only to tell her what he thought of her. She was counting on that; she had every confidence in her ability to make him see reason. She smiled a little in anticipation. Once it was all over he would have to admit that she had done everything from the best of motives. And he would understand. He would forgive her.

She would make him forgive her. She had to, because although it had been her intention to make him fall in love with her, just a little, she knew without doubt that she had fallen head over heels in love with him. It had been impossible not to. He was her match. Her equal. The man she had been waiting for ever since Oliver Hayward had taken her father's money and run.

And they struck sparks off one another, sparks that were all the more potent because although they had both felt the same urgent attraction, they had both been constrained by the situation. Emmy because she had to keep up the pretence until everything was settled . . . and Brodie, well, Brodie had a job to do.

Even so, she thought, they had had a couple of close calls. But it was impossible to do anything, say anything until the decks were cleared, until Kit —

Damn, damn, damn. She banged little clenched fists against her knees. Why on earth had it all been so complicated? If that wretched woman

. . . what was her name? Betty. If Betty hadn't loaned Brodie her car none of this would have been necessary. She would have been away, free.

But Brodie, it seemed, could charm an apple right off a tree. It was just as well he hadn't realised how easily he could have charmed her . . . how easily he could have driven everything from her mind . . .

Or maybe he had. Maybe he was waiting for her to make the first move, admit that she wasn't being entirely honest about Kit.

Or maybe she was just kidding herself.

She absently twisted the ring on her left hand, then, realising what she was doing, she held out her hand to look at it. It was a pretty little thing. She'd seen it in the window of one of those shops that sold second-hand wedding rings and old silver forks and she'd bought it on an impulse. She'd never said it was an engagement ring, or that Kit had bought it for her, but had simply slipped it onto her ring finger and left her father to draw his own conclusions. It had served its purpose well enough, but now she eased it off her finger. The time for deception had passed.

The youth on the other side of the aisle was watching her, apparently fascinated by the flash that even the tiniest diamonds could produce when combined with sunlight. And there was plenty of sunlight. She pushed the ring into her jeans pocket and lifted her hair from her neck, letting the air to her skin.

The bus slowed as it reached the station and she rose quickly, eager to be away, to get everything organised before Brodie showed up — and he would certainly do that, one way or another, before the day was out. She might have set the police on him, but her story had been so outrageous that it would soon be seen for what it was and he would be released.

Then he would be able to conclude his business with all the speed at his command and get on with his holiday. Or maybe not. He could hardly leave her with Kit once he'd bought him off. Could he?

As she swung down from the bus she looked about her, uncertain which way to go. The young man who had been sitting opposite her stumbled as he followed her down the steps, and she put out a hand to help him as he fell against her.

He muttered embarrassed thanks and hurried away. Several other passengers stopped to wish her '*bonne chance*'.

It was her turn to suffer embarrassment, and she too moved quickly away from the bus stop, looking around for a taxi rank, anxious to get to the village as quickly as possible.

★   ★   ★

Once inside the police station Brodie was deprived of all means of harming himself and was left to cool his heels in a cell, presumably while they checked his identity against his passport and his business card. He made no protest at his treatment, remaining polite, calm and co-operative as he answered the officers' questions, aware that bluster and bad temper would only delay things.

Once the police realised that they had been made fools of, they would be only too happy to help him find Miss Emerald Carlisle.

Her story had better be a good one, or he might be tempted to leave her locked up until her father came to bail her out. It was certainly what she deserved, he thought grimly.

* * *

Emmy was hungry. She didn't dare waste time going into a café but, spotting a patisserie she decided to buy something to eat in the taxi. She chose a couple of savoury pastries and asked for a can of soda.

It came to twenty-seven francs. She

didn't have enough change from the bus fare, and put her hand into her other pocket for a hundred-franc note. The woman waited patiently while she searched. Two jeans pockets, no matter how deep, did not take a lot of searching. The notes had gone. And so had the little engagement ring. She remembered the youth stumbling against her at the bus stop and realised, with a sinking heart, that her pocket had been picked as cleanly as a ripe plum.

He had seen her put the ring in her pocket. The money had just been a bonus.

'*Pardon, madame*,' she said, backing away from the counter. '*J'ai perdu ma monnaie . . .* ' Her French, at least, was coming on in leaps and bounds. She hadn't even had to think about that.

There was some sympathetic clucking, but Emmy knew she did not deserve sympathy. She had behaved badly and this setback was no more than her just deserts.

As she turned and walked from the

shop someone called after her, advising her to go to the police station and report her loss. She raised a hand in acknowledgement, but it was hardly an option under the circumstances. Brodie might be locked safely away. On the other hand, he might just be telling the local police all about Emerald Carlisle and what she had done. They would not be amused. Neither would he.

She counted the change in her pocket again. Twenty-two francs, a few centimes. That wouldn't take her very far. All that was left was to telephone the bar in the village and hope Kit was there. Or that someone would go and find him if she could summon up sufficient French to explain how urgent it was, that she was stranded . . . She glanced around, looking for a telephone kiosk, and spotted the post office. There was bound to be one there.

The phone did not take money, only *jetons*. She parted with a few more of her precious francs to buy the tokens and went back to the box. It was only then that she realised the pickpocket had taken her diary too, undoubtedly assuming that it was a wallet. How on earth could he have got away with so much in that quick stumble against her?

She sighed. She'd been told once that a skilled pickpocket could empty a buttoned-down shirt pocket while he looked you right in the eye and smiled. Besides, it didn't really matter how it had been done, what mattered was that she now had no idea of the telephone number of the café.

The dial at the centre of the telephone tantalisingly offered Renseignements. Unfortunately Enquiries would not be able to help since she didn't know the name of the café or the proprietor.

Kit had simply telephoned with the number as a contact point. And she'd only managed to persuade him to do that on the pretext that someone she knew had seen one of his landscapes and wanted to commission him to paint the view from her house.

And there was worse. The directions

to the farmhouse were written in her diary. Without it she would never be able to find the wretched place.

Emmy wandered back out into the late-morning sunshine. It was blisteringly hot, but the air was heavy, threatening, full of electricity. She bought a cold soda from a kiosk, sat on a bench and drank it slowly, trying to decide what to do next. Phone her father? Tell him where she was and that she was stranded without enough money to buy herself a sandwich? Or should she walk across to the police station and throw herself on Brodie's mercy?

She took a franc from her pocket and twisted it round and round in her fingers. Heads or tails?

She didn't need to toss a coin. Her choice had been made the moment he had kissed her. No, before that. The moment he had nearly kissed her. The moment she had known that being kissed by him would be a definitive experience and that ever afterwards anyone else would be an anticlimax. But she didn't intend there should be anyone else.

Across the square a musician was playing a violin exquisitely. He was playing a piece she loved, 'Romance' from *The Gadfly*. On an impulse she got up and crossed the square, dropping every last centime that she had into the hat. Everything that she had. A libation to the gods.

Then she turned towards the police station.

9

Brodie was offered sincere apologies for any inconvenience he might have suffered, coffee and any possible assistance — in that order. He accepted the apologies gracefully, assuring the officers that they had nothing to reproach themselves for.

He declined the coffee; he had already had two cups while he was waiting for his bona fides to be confirmed. As for assistance, he wondered if it would be possible for the police to help him trace an Englishman residing somewhere in the region.

It took no time at all for them to locate the whereabouts of Mr Christopher Fairfax, and furnish Brodie with his address. He was offered an escort to show him the way. He declined. He'd managed to convince the police that this was a lovers' quarrel, that Emmy had taken a step too far. They had been amused, sympathetic and a donation to the police welfare fund had ensured that they would not pursue the matter. He didn't want them present when he finally caught up with Emmy and Kit, or they might have cause to doubt his word. Besides, he'd had quite enough of policemen for one day.

Then as he turned away from the desk he was confronted by the most unexpected sight. Emerald Carlisle, her red curls glowing like a copper halo in the sunlight, walking through the door of the police station.

Some angel.

Yet it was all he could do to prevent himself from going to her, wrapping her in his arms and telling her that it was all right. That he understood. Because he did understand. Not why she had done it, perhaps, but that she had been driven to it by desperation.

'I thought you would be miles away by now,' he said, keeping his distance.

Emmy stopped uncertainly at the

sound of his voice, blinking as her eyes adjusted themselves to the dimmer light after the glare outside. Then she saw him, his face utterly without expression as he faced her. Relief flooded through her that he was free. She made a move towards him, wanting to fling her arms about him and beg him to forgive her. The rigidity of his posture stopped her. No. It would take more than a kiss this time to put things right.

So she lifted her shoulders a touch awkwardly, attempted a wry smile. 'Me too,' she said. It would have been so easy to lie at that moment. To tell him that she had been so full of remorse about what she had done that she had turned back, unable to leave him to the terrible fate she had inflicted upon him. 'I would have been, but I had my pocket picked as I got off the bus.'

'Really?' He was cool. She could hardly blame him. 'And have you come to report this heinous crime to the police? They are incredibly efficient.

Believe me, I have first-hand experience.'

'Brodie — ' she began, then stopped.
She would not plead with him to
understand. 'No.' She pushed a damp
curl back from her forehead. 'No. I
came to confess what I had done to the
police and throw myself on your mercy,
but obviously you've managed to
extricate yourself without my help — '

'I have, with a little help from my
friends. But I should warn you that I'm
feeling a little short in the mercy
department at the moment, Emerald.'
He regarded her with ill-disguised
irritation. 'Why didn't you just phone
Fairfax and ask him to come and fetch
you?'

'The only number I have for him was
in my diary. All that my youthful thief
left me was my handkerchief.'

'Perhaps he suspected that you would
need it when I caught up with you.'

'I'm sorry, Brodie. Truly. I shouldn't
have done it.' He made no move to
meet her halfway. 'Was it dreadful?'

'I've had better mornings,' he said, moving towards the door, leaving her to choose whether to follow him or not. For a moment rebellion threatened, then Emmy turned and followed him. She had no choice. He glanced at her. 'At least you had the sense to tell them the car was stolen. It took the police all of five minutes to call the rental agency and establish that was a lie. After that they were more inclined to believe me — '

'What did you tell them?'

He stopped, turned and looked down at her. 'That I am simply a hard-working solicitor trying my level best to keep a tiresome young woman out of trouble.'

'Oh.' And succeeding rather well, she thought. 'Did they phone my father? To confirm your story,' she added.

'It wasn't necessary. My office was able to reassure them that I wasn't a kidnapper, or a stalker, or whatever story it was that you told them.' Although how long it would take him to live it down when he got back did not bear thinking about. Jenny would have a field day. 'And then, of course, Monsieur Girard was happy to confirm that he'd known me for at least ten years.'

'I am sorry, Brodie. I just couldn't think of any other way.'

'Don't keeping saying you're sorry, Emerald. You'd do it again without a moment's hesitation if you thought you could get away with the car.'

She remembered the awful sick feeling as the police had closed in on him, as the bus had pulled away from the scene, when all she'd wanted to do was go to him. 'No, Brodie, I wouldn't — '

'I realise that you're getting desperate, Emerald. Perhaps it's time you did me the courtesy of explaining what exactly you're so desperate about. Over lunch?' he offered. 'Since you skipped breakfast.'

His formality was chilling. The way he had started calling her 'Emerald'.

Well, what else had she expected? It could have been worse; it could have been 'Miss Carlisle'. One thing was certain: he wasn't about to hug her and tell her how glad he was to see her. Right now he was probably wishing he had never set eyes on her, and she could hardly blame him.

'Thank you,' she said. 'But actually I'm not feeling very hungry.'

'There's no need to be pathetic, Emerald. I'm not going to beat you.'

'I'm not being pathetic,' she said, with a flash of fire. 'I'm not hungry.' And it was true. Her stomach was in knots of anguish. She climbed into the car and quickly wound down the window to let out the suffocatingly hot air. The musician on the other side of the square had stopped playing. He had packed away his violin and was picking the coins out of his hat. So much for her libation. Perhaps the gods had taken offence at the *jetons*, although surely even violinists must need to make phone calls. She turned to Brodie as he climbed in beside her. 'And I never for a moment thought you would beat me.' And then some tiny devil inside her prompted her to add, 'Just put me over your knee. Or something like that. Wasn't that what you said?'

His eyes darkened, dangerously. 'My God, Emmy — ' Then, clearly regretting the outburst, he said simply, 'You would try the patience of a saint.'

Satisfied that she had at least broken through the ice, she smiled at him. 'You're no saint, Brodie, although I realise that you've been trying very hard to give that impression.' Her reward was to see his fingers shaking, just a little, as he fitted the key to the ignition and started the engine. 'Where are we going?'

'The police, in an effort to recompense me for the discomfort of the past hour or so, have gone out of their way to be helpful. Fortunately for both of us they have managed to discover the whereabouts of Mr Fairfax. I think the sooner we go and talk to him, get this nonsense over with, the better. Don't you?'

'I've been trying to get to him ever since I climbed out of the nursery window, Brodie. But I promise you, it isn't nonsense. If you'd only agreed to let me have a few minutes alone with him before you put my father's proposition to him, I wouldn't have run away this morning.'

'Why?' He turned briefly to look at her. 'What are you going to promise him? Double whatever your father is prepared to pay to get rid of him?'

Her face flamed. 'Do you really think I'd do that?' she exploded, angrily. 'After Oliver?'

'I don't know what you'd do, Emmy. Whatever would most upset your father, I suspect.'

'This isn't anything to do with my father.'

'Isn't it? Aren't you determined to marry a man you know your father will disapprove of simply to spite him for the way he broke up your romance with Hayward?'

'No!' She was shocked that he could think such a thing. 'It isn't like that. Honestly.'

'Honestly? Then why don't you tell me what it *is* like?' he suggested, rather more gently. 'Maybe I can help.'

'I can't. And if I did explain you wouldn't be able to help. You couldn't. Don't you see, Brodie? I'm just trying to do my best for everybody.'

'Then God help us all if you ever decide to do your worst.'

She turned to face the road. 'I really don't want to talk about it any more.'

He shrugged, swallowed a yawn. 'Whatever you say.' As they reached a crossroads he fished a piece of paper out of his shirt pocket and consulted it before turning left. 'Are you any good at navigating?' he asked, handing it to her.

'You'd trust me?'

'I'm simply assuming that you're as tired of these games as I am.' Another yawn crept up on him.

'Are you all right, Brodie?' Emmy asked, finally noticing the dark hollows beneath his eyes. 'Do you want me to drive?'

'No, I don't want you to drive,' he snapped. 'I want you to navigate.'

'Your halo is slipping,' she said, then when he refused to respond she shrugged and consulted the sheet of paper. 'This is written in French.'

'That's because it was written by a Frenchman. Didn't they teach the language at your school?'

'They must have done. I just don't seem to recall going to any of the lessons. I think we turn left just up here.'

'You think?'

'Left, definitely.'

'So long as you're sure,' he said, with heavy irony.

'There should be a signpost.' There was. Vindicated, she made a little bow.

'Don't get carried away, Emmy. We've miles to go yet.'

261

'Kilometres,' she corrected. 'How many?'

'You've got the directions; work it out for yourself.' He glanced at her. 'Are you beginning to wish you'd taken me up on my offer of lunch?'

'Mmm. Still we could stop in the village,' she said hopefully. 'I know there's a café there. It's where I leave messages for Kit.'

'Did you leave one the night we stayed at my flat?'

'Only to say that I was on my way. He might not have got it, if he hasn't been into the village. Perhaps we should stop there anyway and check whether he's left a message for me.'

'He seems a somewhat tepid lover.' She didn't reply.

'Don't worry, Emmy, I won't let you starve. I didn't have much breakfast myself. And I could do with something long and cold.' He wiped his sleeve across his forehead and peered up at the sky. It had lost that clear, deep blue, become murky and threatening.

They drove on for a while through rugged hills, woods, and mellow, rolling farmland splashed with russets and sharp greens. And always in the distance, first ahead of them, then shifting to the right as the road veered away, was the evocative marbled ridge of Montagne Ste Victoire.

It was early afternoon by the time they pulled up in front of a small café in the village square. It had to be the one. There was only one. They went inside to get away from the relentless heat and Brodie asked for two citron pressés and a large bottle of mineral water.

Emmy left the talking to him. She was just too hot, too exhausted to even think about Kit.

'The *patron* is asking his wife to make us a couple of omelettes,' he said, joining her at a table.

'Fine.'

'Fairfax hasn't been here for days.'

'Great.' She put her head down on her arms. 'Is it always this hot?'

'I think it's probably building up to a

storm.' She groaned. 'Don't tell me, you're scared of thunder.'

She managed a grin from beneath her curls. 'I had a series of perfectly bloody nannies, Brodie, each of whom made a point of passing on her own particular neurosis. But actually it's not thunder that bothers me. At least, not much. It's lightning. Nanny number six hundred and thirty-two knew someone who had been struck by it.' She sat up and drew a finger dramatically across her throat. 'Fried to a crisp.'

Brodie regarded her doubtfully. 'That's quite a line in bedtime stories.'

'It certainly makes Beatrix Potter appear rather tame,' she agreed. 'Although I seem to remember something about a fierce, bad rabbit. He got blasted by a hunter with a shotgun so that only his tail and whiskers were left.'

'You're kidding me?'

'No, I swear it. Her stories weren't all sweet and innocent, you know. Just look what happened to Peter Rabbit's father.'

Brodie, who had been spared these bloodthirsty tales as an infant, was curious. 'What happened to him?'

'He was put into a pie. Oh, look, here comes our food.' Omelettes, salad, bread and a bowl of local olives were spread on the table. 'It looks wonderful.'

Brodie spoke to the *patron*. Emmy, her ears becoming attuned to the language, picked up a little of what was said. 'Is there going to be a storm?' she asked.

'There's one forecast for late tonight, but apparently the forecasters have been promising it for a week so he's not holding his breath.'

'What do you think?'

'I'm a lawyer, Emmy; forecasting the weather is as much a mystery to me as it seems to be to the meteorologists. But I don't think we'll linger over this.' He picked up a fork and broke his omelette.

'That's reassuring,' Emmy said, following suit.

'If you've got a better plan I'm perfectly happy to listen to it.'

'No. We've come this far; we might as well get it over with.' She reached for the pepper grinder.

Brodie beat her to it, catching her hand. 'What happened to your engagement ring, Emmy?'

'It was picked, along with my money and my diary,' she said, flippantly.

'From your finger?' he asked, concerned, and was surprised to see the faint flush of colour rise to her cheeks.

'No, it was a bit loose. I put it in my pocket.'

'You must have been distraught when you realised it was gone,' he said evenly. 'You really should have reported it to the police or your insurance company might be difficult about covering the loss.'

'I hadn't got around to insuring it,' she mumbled.

It was doubtful if her insurance company would have believed her if she had, he thought. Women like Emerald

Carlisle wore diamonds worth thousands of pounds. Or in Miss Carlisle's case surely an emerald would have been the stone of choice? An emerald flanked with diamonds. She certainly didn't seem to be desperately upset at the loss of the ring Kit Fairfax had given her. And he was quite certain that, no matter how tiny it was, she would have been distraught to lose a ring given her as a promise of love.

'Finished? Can I get you anything else?'

'No. I just need to go and freshen up; I won't be a moment.'

'Take as long as you like, Emmy. But if you decide to do a disappearing trick I'll turn around and drive straight back to Marseilles. And the car is locked, if you were thinking you might get away with your bags.'

'I wasn't. There wouldn't be any point. You know where Kit is now, Brodie, and you'd get there before me. I know when I'm beaten.'

He watched her as she turned and

walked away. Did she? Really? Somehow he doubted that. Half a chance, less, was all she'd need and he'd be the one left to find his own way home.

He took out his mobile and dialled Mark Reed. 'There's no need to spend any more time on this case, Mark; I've found out where Kit Fairfax is staying.'

'Staying is right. Apparently his father, a Frenchman by the name of Savarin, died recently, and young Mr Fairfax has inherited his farmhouse in Provence, a vineyard, an olive grove and considerable acres of very pretty countryside, along with some very nice property on the coast. According to the diary correspondent I spoke to, he has no intention of returning to England in the immediate future. All in the nick of time, because the lease on that studio of his was about to run out.'

Something prickled at the back of Brodie's mind. 'Why didn't he ask his father for help with that?'

'I understand they hadn't spoken for years. The father walked out on the mother — a common enough story — and when his mother reverted to her own name — Fairfax — the boy did too.'

'The son refused to acknowledge the father, but under French law the father couldn't disinherit his son.'

'So I understand. Maybe the Honourable Gerald won't be quite so disappointed with his daughter's choice after all. I wonder why she didn't tell him?'

'Who knows? Maybe she just wanted her father to accept the man she loved, no matter how unsuitable he seemed. Thanks for your help, Mark. I won't forget it.'

'Neither will the Honourable Gerald. My bill for services rendered promises to be memorable.'

Brodie stared out through the café door, seeing nothing. Something Mark Reed had said was important. He pressed his fingers against his eyes, rubbing them hard. If only he wasn't so damned tired.

'I'm ready, Brodie.'

269

He looked up to see Emmy standing in front of him. 'Oh, right. Let's go, then.' He paid the *patron* and led the way out of the café.

They turned off the narrow paved road that led from the village and had been climbing steadily for about twenty minutes along a country track carved into the hillside, its sandstone slabs worn away by cartwheels, when the first fat raindrop splashed on the windscreen, stirring the dust.

'How much further?' Emmy asked nervously, peering up through the windscreen at a sky that seemed to have darkened in seconds. A few sheep grazing on the hillside above them began to shift nervously, moving into a huddle around a little stone shelter.

'You've got the instructions,' he reminded her. 'But once we're on the other side of the hill we should be able to see the farm.' He hoped.

He used the washers on the windscreen and for a moment or two nothing happened. Then without warning the rain began to fall in a sudden torrent, cutting visibility by half as the weather closed in and the wipers struggled to keep up with the downpour.

Within minutes thick gouts of red muddy water were spilling off the hillside onto the road, churning up the loose dust on the surface and washing it away as the flood continued on down the hill.

Brodie's hands tightened on the wheel as potholes that had been filled with loose earth were washed out and the car began to bounce and shift on the uneven surface. Emmy clutched at her seat and fervently prayed that there would be no lightning. Neither of them mentioned turning back. There was nowhere to turn on the narrow track.

'Maybe we should stop,' Emmy suggested nervously. 'Just until it eases.'

'This could last for hours.'

She groaned. 'It's all my fault. We could have been here hours ago. Yesterday, even, if I hadn't lied about flying — ' She broke off with a little scream as lightning flashed behind the hill swiftly followed by a low rumble of thunder. Brodie stopped the car and turned to her.

'Emmy, sweetheart — ' he began, but another, more vivid flash had her diving into his arms, hiding her face in his shoulder.

'Hold me, Brodie. I can't bear it.'

She was trembling against him. She might have lied about her fear of flying, but this was real enough. He unfastened his seatbelt and then hers, pulling her into his lap to hold her, cradling her against him, covering her with his body as he murmured softly against her hair, against her neck. Words of comfort, words of love that he knew she could not hear.

The noise was unbelievable. A fierce tattoo of rain, gusts of wind that rocked the car so that she made tiny, mindless sounds against his chest. And then there was the thunder, moving closer with each succeeding flash of lightning, each time a little louder, until a crack directly above them seemed to match the lightning and split the sky. And the rain continued like an impenetrable wall of water.

Emmy was whimpering against him, clawing at him with her hands so that he was forced to capture them, tuck them against his chest so that he could hold her tightly. She was beyond reason and he couldn't blame her. Faced with the uncontrollable forces of nature, anyone who said they were not scared would be lying.

Something heavy hit the top of the car, denting it so that the roof caved in behind them, but, worse, shifting the back end round where the ground had been washed from beneath the wheels.

'What was that?' Emmy cried out, her nails digging through his shirt.

A sheep. It must have lost its footing on the slope above them. He'd seen the poor creature as it had rolled on down the hillside. 'Nothing. The branch of a tree,' he told her. If anything the rain was coming down harder, and as the car shifted again, sliding towards the downward slope, he knew they would have to make a move, one way or another. He glanced at the girl cowering in his arms. He would have to make the choice. Start the car and try and drive on, or get out before they joined the sheep in the bottom of the gully.

Not much of a choice. Driving was near to impossible with visibility not more than a yard in front of him. If the road had been washed out ahead of them he would never see it. And Emmy was close to hysteria.

'Emmy.' He gave her a little shake. 'We've got to get out of here,' he shouted above the noise of the storm.

★ ★ ★

She didn't appear to hear him. 'Darling, please . . . ' It was no use. The daring girl who had shimmied two floors down a drainpipe without turning a hair was now quite unable to help herself.

He released the door catch and the door was immediately whipped away from him by the wind, banging hard against the bank. He didn't bother to shout any more. He half leaned, half fell out of the car with Emmy, dragging her clear, holding onto her as the back slewed round with a rending of metal as the underside dragged against the lip of the road and slipped over the edge.

It remained there, poised, rocking for a moment. Emmy screamed as it slipped another foot or so, but then it stuck, caught on a tree stump, or a rock perhaps. Whatever, it wouldn't stay there for long.

Emmy, shivering with terror and now with cold, was already soaked to the skin, her jeans and T-shirt, already mud-splattered, clinging to her. 'Wait here,' he shouted, pushing her back against the bank. 'Don't move.'

She stared at him as if unable to comprehend what he was saying, wide-eyed, terrified, the rain pouring down her face, her red hair plastered against her head, the white skin almost transparent at her temple. He knew then that he loved her, would die for her if need be, but this was not the moment for crazy declarations of love. Instead he bent down and kissed her, hard, on the mouth.

Emmy momentarily forgot the storm, her terror; all she felt was the heat that surged through her as Brodie kissed her. But even as she made to grab him, hold him by the shirt-front and kiss him back, he turned away and dived across the road towards the car.

'Brodie!' Her voice was dashed away by the wind and he didn't hear it. 'I love you, Brodie,' she shouted. He half turned, as if her words had finally penetrated the noise of the storm, but without warning the ground beneath him gave way and he disappeared from sight.

10

Emmy flung herself to the ground and crawled across the road to the edge. 'Brodie,' she called, her voice hoarse, her breath blown away by the wind. 'Please come back. Oh, darling, please don't be hurt. I love you so much. I should have told you.'

His face suddenly appeared just below her. There was a smear of mud across his cheek and the rain was dripping over his dark brows, down his nose and running off his chin. He dashed it away with his shirtsleeve, but the torrent was so strong that it made little impression. 'I thought I told you to stay over there,' he said, gasping a little as he fought for breath. But down at ground level, protected by the bulk of the car, the wind wasn't so strong.

'I thought you'd fallen. I thought — ' She hesitated, aware that she had exposed raw feelings that she needed to examine, think about. Had he heard her? There was nothing in his expression to suggest that he had.

'What did you think, Emmy?' She shook her head and after a moment he shrugged. 'I was just rescuing your bag before the car fell down there into the river.' He held out his hand to help her down. 'Come on, there's a hut — '

She slapped away his hand, scrambling to her feet. 'My bag? You risked your life for a few clothes?' She couldn't believe a man could be so stupid. She loved him! How dared he risk his life when she loved him? 'You stupid, idiotic . . . ' she struggled for a suitably scathing insult ' . . . *man!*' she yelled at him as anger obliterated all fear of the thunder still crashing around the hills, the distant flashes of lightning. 'How could you?'

He pulled himself up onto the road. 'A simple thank you would have done,' he said, when he was certain she was finished.

But she wasn't finished with him. She was far from finished. 'Thank you?' She glared down at him. 'You expect me to thank you? What would I have told your mother if the car had come down on top of you, Brodie? That you died because I couldn't survive without a change of clothes?' She swung angrily, flinging her fist at his shoulder. 'What kind of a mindless bimbo do you think I am?' She swung again, but evidently he had had enough because he moved and she missed.

She let out a yell as her feet went from beneath her and she found herself sliding on her bottom down a mudslide. Then she had no breath to waste on anything so trivial as yelling for help. Every time she managed to grab a mouthful of air it was knocked right out of her again.

But Brodie came after her anyway, grabbing at her T-shirt to slow her, pulling her over onto him as they bumped and bounced over the uneven ground so that he took the worst of the

pounding. Eventually the ground lev-
elled out and they slithered to a halt in
a tangle of arms and legs.

For a moment they stared at one
another, breathless, grinning a little at
the crazy roller-coaster ride they had
just taken and survived. 'Let's go back
and do that again, Brodie,' Emmy said
finally as her heart began to return to
something like normal.

Brodie's smile faded. 'I've got a much
better idea.' She was poised above him,
her hips pressed against his. She didn't
need a phrasebook to interpret his
meaning, and suddenly her heart rate
was back in the stratosphere.

The rain hammering down on them
washed away the worst of the mud and
as he carefully lifted the strands of hair
away from her mouth, her cheeks, his
touch sent fingers of heat racing
through her, a new, rare heat that sent
her spirits soaring, her pulse hammering in her ears. There were moments,
perfect moments in life, that were a
special gift and she knew without a

doubt that this was one of them.

And because of everything that had happened, because of Kit and her father and because she recognised that Brodie was in a situation that made it impossible for him to make the first move, she would have to take the lead.

His eyes never left hers as she pushed the black strands of hair back from his forehead, as she lightly touched a graze where a stone had caught his cheek, as she ran her hands down his throat. But they grew darker, luminous with desire.

But he made no move as she slowly unbuttoned his shirt, pushing it back so that the rain poured over his naked chest, lowering her head to touch his slick golden skin with her lips. No move, but she felt the sudden catch in his breath, the vibration of a low growl deep in his throat as her teeth teased momentarily at his small male nipples, a growl that intensified as the tip of her tongue swirled in the hollows of his neck.

Suddenly desperate to feel the rain

on her own naked skin, she sat up, raised her arms and pulled her ruined T-shirt over her head. Then she reached behind to unfasten her bra, and when it swung free held the tiny scrap of lace at arm's length and let it fall.

She felt him shudder with suppressed desire as she swayed forward until the taut peaks of her breasts touched him. But still he held her only with his eyes as, slowly, she lowered her mouth to his.

She made no immediate move to kiss him, but touched the sensuous curve of his lower lip with her tongue.

It was running with rainwater and she took it between her own lips, sipping from it like a hummingbird taking nectar from a flower. Then she dipped her tongue into his mouth, and after that the question of who was taking the lead was no longer a question that either of them was interested in.

There was just an urgency to be free of clinging denim, wet, muddy cotton chinos, to feel skin against skin, and for long moments they hungrily explored each other with hands and lips until Brodie, ignoring Emmy's cries of protest as he stopped kissing her for a moment, picked her up and carried her towards the dry stone shepherd's hut.

It was dark inside the *borie*, but dry, and much warmer out of the wind. And the ground was thickly covered in a bed of dried heather and herbs that smelt sweet as they lay down together.

'Brodie,' Emmy began, her voice sounding unnaturally loud in the sudden silence away from the wind. But he covered her lips, first with his fingers and then with his lips, and after that there was no need for words. The moment was perfect, the man was perfect and she loved him. That was all that mattered. Explanations would wait. Everything would sort itself out. Later.

★ ★ ★

Emmy woke to a golden light edging around the door of the *borie*. She eased herself from Brodie's arms and knelt up to look out. The storm had passed and the sun was making everything steam. She eased her head out of the door, the brilliant light making her very conscious of her nakedness, but there was no one about, and spotting her bag lying a few yards away, she made a dash for it.

Brodie hadn't stirred, didn't move as she pulled on not quite dry pants and a crumpled dress.

She knelt down beside him, put out a finger to touch his cheek and then hesitated, remembering the tired hollows beneath his eyes, in his cheeks. Two nights' sleeping on a sofa had taken its toll. She wouldn't disturb him. Instead she pulled the baggy rugby shirt she wore at night out of her bag and tucked it round him.

She sat for a while, smiling, as she watched the even rise and fall of his breathing. His hair had dried in rumpled curls and she was unable to resist the temptation to tease one out, see it spring back. 'Oh, Brodie, darling Brodie,' she murmured. 'I do love you so much.'

He didn't stir. She glanced at her watch, tilting it towards the slightly open door so that she could see the time. It was just after five. They should be moving soon or it would get dark, and she had no idea how far they would have to walk.

She wondered what had happened to the directions to the farmhouse. She had been reading them when the storm had started. Had she dropped them? Or pushed them into her jeans pocket? She rose quietly and let herself out of the hut. Their clothes were scattered where they had torn them off, and, blushing just a little at the memory of her wanton behaviour, she gathered them up. The paper was not in her pocket.

She dropped the clothes inside the hut door and climbed up to the road where the car remained, wedged against a large rock at a crazy angle to the sky. The floor of the car by the front seats was on a level with her head, and, peering through the open door on the driver's side, she saw the piece of paper he had given her where it had fallen as he had pulled her into his arms. She reached across and caught it between outstretched fingers, jumping back quickly as the car seemed to rock a little.

She looked at the directions and realised the farmhouse wasn't very far. Less than a kilometre, according to the directions the police had given him. She looked along the road; it was steaming as it dried out in the sun. She looked back at the hut.

She could be at the farmhouse in ten minutes. She would be back with Kit and a truck to pull the car back onto the road before Brodie had woken up. It would be something to make up for what she had done this morning. She blew a kiss back towards the *borie* and then turned and hurried towards the farmhouse.

* ★ *

Brodie stirred. His body felt as if it had been in a concrete mixer but he didn't care. He felt warm and fulfilled and quite unbelievably happy. He turned to Emmy, planning to wake her with a kiss, pull her into his arms and tell her just how much he loved her. But Emmy wasn't there.

For a moment it didn't sink in.

He shrugged off the rugby shirt and then pulled it over his head. He saw her bag, open where she had rifled through it for something to wear. He saw the pile of wet clothes by the door, fished out damp boxer shorts, soggy shoes and stepped into them before going outside.

'Emmy,' he called. The ground was steaming and it was like looking through a golden mist. 'Emmy?' But there was no answer. She had gone. And his blood ran cold as he realised where she had gone. And Tom Brodie let out a loud, animal bellow as pain and anger washed over him.

Selfish, spoilt, determined to get her own way, she had tried everything to shake free of him. Each time he had found it so easy to forgive her, to understand. Even this morning, locked up in the police station, he hadn't believed it was personal, had been so sure that once he saw her with Kit it would all fall into place and he would know exactly what she was up to.

But now she had used him and betrayed him. Now it felt very personal, and whatever happened in the next few hours he was determined that Miss Emerald Carlisle would not get her own way. And once he had dealt with Kit Fairfax he would make it his business to see that she suffered for what she had done.

He looked down at himself. First he would change into dry clothes. He wasn't about to confront either of them looking like a refugee from some disaster.

His own bag was still in the car, and he climbed back up to the road. Then he stripped off, rubbed himself clean with the rugby shirt and dressed in a fresh shirt, the lightweight suit he had worn on the train — trousers neatly sponged and pressed by Madame Girard — and a pair of clean, dry shoes. He knotted a tie about his neck and combed his hair.

Not quite his usual standard of grooming for a business meeting, but it would have to do. Then he took his briefcase from the rear seat and slammed the door irritably behind him before setting off down the road towards the farm.

Behind him there was a rending of metal, a crash as the rock propping the Renault in place finally succumbed to the undermining effects of the rain, the weight of the car and gravity.

Brodie did not even turn around.

He wasn't sure how far he would have to walk, but reasoned, if Emerald had decided it was worth taking the risk of running for it, it couldn't be that far. It wasn't. After about half a mile the track curved round the hill and he saw the farmhouse below him. It was grey stone, the roof that wonderful mottled mixture of faded pink and brown rounded tiles that looked like knitting, the ridge like some crooked seam.

Behind it a cypress tree provided a dark exclamation point, in front there was a neat courtyard that suggested careful husbandry. And away to the right neat rows of olive trees, leaves silvering as the remnants of the storm's wind lifted them gently.

Fairfax had inherited a well-cared-for and prosperous estate. It would take more than a hundred thousand pounds to buy him. But perhaps Mark Reed was right. Maybe money, property would be all that was needed to change Gerald Carlisle's mind, Brodie thought coldly, when love had been unable to move him.

How on earth had he come to believe that the daughter was so different from the father? They were cut from the same cloth — wilful, selfish people who cared for nothing or no one, only getting their own way.

He crossed the courtyard, rapped at the open door and walked in without waiting for an invitation. Emerald Carlisle and Kit Fairfax turned, startled, wine glasses in their hands. There was a suitcase by the door.

'I've obviously arrived in the very nick of time,' he said. 'You shouldn't have wasted time toasting your great escape.'

'Brodie!' Emmy exclaimed, putting down her glass and rushing across to him. 'We were just coming to fetch you in the Jeep. Kit is going to pull the car back onto the road — '

'The car is down at the bottom of the gully. It will take more than a Jeep to get it up.'

'Would you like a glass of wine, Mr Brodie?' Kit offered.

'It's a little soon to celebrate, surely?' he said, his voice like chipped ice. 'Let's get the formalities over with first.' He walked across to the huge scrubbed table that dominated the kitchen and placed his briefcase on it, taking out the file that Carlisle had given him. 'Would you care to sit down, Mr Fairfax? This shouldn't take long.'

'Brodie . . . ' Emmy began uncertainly. She took a step towards him. 'Tom?' She put her hand out to touch his arm. 'What's wrong?' She glanced at the suitcase by the door. 'Surely you don't think . . . ? I was coming straight back . . . '

He was used to hiding his feelings, but it took all his will-power to keep his face from betraying all the pain, all the hurt. 'I'm sure you were. Once you had got what you wanted — your five minutes with Fairfax to make sure he understood exactly what he had to do.'

'No . . . darling . . . '

Darling? What more did she want from him, for heaven's sake? She had his heart, his mind and finally his body. Did she want his soul, too? He stared down at her, then pointedly at the hand on his arm. She snatched it back as if her fingers had suddenly been burnt.

'Fairfax?' he said, turning to the fair-haired young man watching this interchange with a perplexed expression. 'I'd like to get on with this.' Kit, his boyish face crumpled in consternation at his visitor's tone, glanced at Emmy. But she was no help, staring at Brodie as if she couldn't believe her ears. Brodie shrugged. He was perfectly willing to conduct business on his feet if necessary. 'I have no doubt that Emerald has already explained the purpose of this visit.' He didn't wait for confirmation. 'Gerald Carlisle is of the opinion that you are not a suitable husband for his daughter — '

'But Emmy said — '

Brodie was in no mood to listen to what Emmy had said. 'And he has authorised me to offer you a sum of one hundred thousand pounds,' he continued as if Fairfax had not spoken, 'on the understanding that you will with-draw from the scene and never see her again.' He produced a sheet of paper that Carlisle had provided for the man's signature. 'Sign this and the cheque will be immediately drawn in whatever currency you prefer.'

Fairfax had the kind of skin that flushed crimson when he was angry or embarrassed. It was crimson now. 'I don't believe I'm hearing this,' he said.

It was anger, Brodie noted.

'Does that mean you were expecting more? I dare say he would go a little higher. A hundred and twenty?' he suggested. 'It's a very generous offer — '

'You bastard!' Fairfax took a step forward and swung. The move was so unexpected that although he saw it coming Brodie didn't react. Instead he watched the man's arm swing up and round as if in slow motion.

Then the fist at the end of the arm connected with his chin, knocking him clean off his feet, hurtling him back against the sink, jarring his back. Dazed, unable to prevent himself from falling, he slid down onto the floor and for a moment lay there as he tried to come to terms with what had happened.

Was that a refusal? Suppose he told the man about the way he and Emmy had made love, tearing at each other's clothes as the rain had poured over them, lost to everything but desire . . .

No. Oh, God, no. He couldn't do that to her. Even now. He closed his eyes.

'Tom! Tom, darling . . . ' Emmy darted forward, flinging herself to her knees, cradling his head in her lap. She smelt of Chanel and rainwater and the love they had shared, and all he wanted to do was hold her, tell her how much he loved her. Because he couldn't hate her. He would never hate her, no matter what she did.

'Get me some water, Kit, quickly.' He felt her lips press against his brow. 'Tom, dear Tom, please wake up.' She took the water from Kit, dipped her fingers in the glass and rubbed them over his forehead. 'I'm not going to marry Kit. I was never going to marry him — '

He opened his eyes. 'Never?'

She stared down at him. 'You weren't unconscious,' she said, accusingly.

'Just resting my eyes. Tell me about Kit.' Then suddenly it all fell into place and he knew. 'No, there's no need. It was the money, wasn't it? You just wanted him to have the money so he could buy the lease of his studio.' He struggled to sit up. 'But why was it so important that you talked to him before I did?'

'Because he didn't know anything about it. If Hollingworth didn't treat me like a three-year-old, refusing to let me have more than pocket money — but I'm just a stupid, feeble girl who can't be trusted — I wouldn't have had to do this — '

'So you remembered what happened when you ran away with Oliver

Hayward and decided to try it again. If you couldn't use your own money, you'd get your father to bail the man out?' He laughed. 'Betty was right.'

'Betty?'

'She told me that nothing was what it seemed.'

'Oh.'

'Emmy! Is that true?' Kit demanded. 'You pretended . . . ? I can't believe you could do something so dreadful.'

'Dreadful? What was so dreadful about it?' she demanded. 'If my father hadn't had me followed after he saw our picture in *Tatler* at that charity thing it would never have occurred to me.'

'That's why you asked me to paint your portrait, isn't it?'

Emmy grinned. 'How else was I going to spend all those afternoons at your studio?'

'And why you insisted on sleeping on my sofa, going on about having too much to drink at lunchtime when you scarcely touch a drop?'

'Sorry,' she said.

'So you should be.'

'I know. But my father is a rich man, and he doesn't do nearly enough to support the arts . . . '

Brodie began to laugh. 'All that plotting and planning, for nothing.'

'No,' Emmy said. 'It doesn't have to be for nothing. He can still have the money. You won't say anything, will you, darling? Please, Tom. My father expects you to settle with Kit. He'll be pleased with you . . . '

'But I don't need it, Emmy,' Kit explained. 'I have this farmhouse and some property down at the coast. That's where I was going when you turned up. I've got a meeting with a lawyer about selling a villa.'

'A *what*?'

'A villa. One of three my father left me. In fact if it hadn't been for the storm you'd have missed me.' He glanced at his watch. 'Look, why don't you two make yourselves at home here? I'll be back tomorrow.' He glanced at

Emmy and Brodie. 'No, not tomorrow,' he said hurriedly. 'It'll be the weekend at least. I'll stop at the village, Brodie, and sort out something about the car on my way. Just leave the key under the flowerpot when you leave.'

Brodie raised a hand to acknowledge that he'd heard. His mouth was too busy kissing Emmy.

* * *

'Brodie!' Emmy's urgent whisper brought Brodie drifting up from sleep and he half opened his eyes, smiling into her morning face. Her curls were tumbled about her cheeks, her green-gold slumberous eyes were full of love.

'Hi, sweetheart,' he said softly, then, suddenly and urgently wide awake, he pulled her down to him and kissed her. For a moment she protested, mumbling something beneath his mouth, but, laughing, he turned her onto her back. 'Oh, no. When you wake up a man, my darling, you have to pay a forfeit,' he said. 'Now, then, what will it be?'

'Brodie — '

'I thought, last night, that we'd agreed you'd call me Tom,' he said, kissing her shoulder. 'Now that we're better acquainted.'

'Tom — '

'That's better. Now this forfeit . . . A kiss, here, perhaps?' He grazed her throat with his mouth. 'Or here? Or here?' He eased down her body, liberally planting kisses over her shoulders, her breasts, her stomach, and for a moment she relaxed, giggling as the night stubble of his chin tickled and tormented her delicate skin.

Then her body stiffened beneath him. 'Tom!' she said, and there was something about the urgency with which she said the name that made him stop, look up.

But Emerald wasn't looking at him, she was looking towards the door. He turned, and in the entrance were framed the shocked faces of Gerald Carlisle and James Hollingworth.

'I was going to tell you,' Emmy said faintly, 'that I thought I heard someone downstairs. It was why I woke you up. But I forgot.'

Gerald Carlisle looked as if he was about to have a stroke.

'Would you mind telling me what the devil you think you're doing, Brodie?' he demanded.

For one delicious moment Tom Brodie considered the obvious, then discarded it. 'I'm carrying out your instructions,' he said. 'You did say that I was to use whatever means were necessary to prevent Emerald from marrying Kit Fairfax?'

Gerald Carlisle stared at him. Then at his daughter. 'I give up,' he said. 'Do what you want. You've made your bed once too often, my girl. Well, now you can lie on it.'

Brodie raised one darkly defined brow at Emmy, who was clutching the sheet to her neck. 'You heard the man, sweetheart. Lie down. I'll be right with you.'

Emmy gasped, catching her lower lip between her teeth to stop herself from laughing out loud at her father's outraged expression. Then she slid back down against the pillows. Brodie, his face expressionless, turned to Carlisle and Hollingworth.

'As you can see, gentlemen, the lady has made her choice. Please shut the door on your way out.'

★ ★ ★

Tom Brodie regarded the man sitting behind the ornate desk and waited. He could afford to be patient. He held all the cards — a fact he was sure that Gerald Carlisle was quite aware of.

'What exactly do you want from me, Brodie?' he asked finally. 'I mean, a hundred thousand pounds isn't going to shift you, is it?'

'No, but if you've got that kind of money looking for a good home I can suggest a couple of worthy causes that would be grateful for the help.'

'How much?' he replied bluntly.

Brodie didn't lose his temper. He was being tested. He'd expected that. 'I only want your daughter. And your blessing.'

'So you came to ask for her hand in marriage like some old-fashioned suitor?' Gerald Carlisle didn't sound convinced.

'I thought that was how gentlemen did it. I would have given you chapter and verse of my family history and my prospects, too, but I imagine you've already had James Hollingworth down here to lay it out in words of one syllable.' Hollingworth had already told him as much. 'In your shoes, that's what I would do.'

'Oh, you would, would you?' He paused. 'Well, I have. And the man had the nerve to tell me Emmy was lucky to find you.'

Brodie buried his grin. James Hollingworth hadn't told him that. 'We found each other. And I think I'm the lucky one.'

'I'm sure you do.' He glared at Tom.

303

'If you do get married, where will you live? Emerald's flat isn't big enough — '

'Mine is.'

'A converted warehouse on the wrong side of the river?' He was dismissive. 'No. You'll need a house. I suppose it had better be my wedding present. I'll get my agent — '

'All in good time.'

'But — '

'We can find our own house. When we're ready to move. And I'll pay for it.'

Gerald Carlisle, already reaching for the telephone, paused. Then, quite suddenly, his face softened and he began to laugh. 'By God, Brodie, Emmy met her match when she crossed your path. Whatever else it is, your married life won't be dull.'

Suddenly recognising in Gerald Carlisle a father who cared desperately about his daughter, wanting nothing bad to happen to her, ever, Brodie found himself responding with an unexpected warmth to the man. 'No, I don't suppose it will be. But love should never be dull. And I do love her. I'll do everything I can to make her happy.'

'Will you?' Carlisle rose. 'Then I suppose all that's left is to set the date and have a drink.'

As Tom stood up to take the hand extended to him Emmy burst into the room. 'Darlings, it's all fixed. The vicar is reading the banns on Sunday and the wedding will be on the last Saturday in September — '

'*This* September?' Gerald Carlisle was stunned.

'Well, we could have waited until October . . . ' She slipped her arm through her father's and looked up at him. 'But your diary is solid with shooting parties all through October *and* November. Then it's Christmas, and I absolutely refuse to get married in the middle of winter . . . ' She gave a little shiver. 'The photographs would be all mud and gooseflesh.' She turned wide gold-green eyes on Tom and linked her other arm with his. 'Of course, if you think it's too much trouble I suppose we could forget all the formalities and just elope — '

'September's just fine with me, Emmy,' her father intervened hurriedly. 'Tom?'

But Tom was smiling at Emmy. 'If that's the earliest we can manage . . . '

'Do you think Betty will come?' Emmy asked.

'We'll stop by on the way home and ask her.'

Gerald Carlisle considered asking who Betty might be, but decided against it. Instead he crossed to the phone. 'I suppose I'd better ask Mrs Johnson to bring up a bottle of champagne,' he said, trying very hard not to smile too much. Then he paused as Emmy wound her arms around Tom Brodie's neck, raising herself on tiptoe to kiss him. 'Perhaps, on second thoughts, *I'd* better go and get it . . . ' he murmured. But he was talking to himself.